The Man
From The Clouds

J. STORER CLOUSTON

1st WORLD
LIBRARY
Literary Society

The Man From The Clouds

J. STORER CLOUSTON

© 1st World Library – Literary Society, 2004
PO Box 2211
Fairfield, IA 52556
www.1stworldlibrary.org
First Edition

LCCN: 2004091220

Softcover ISBN: 1-59540-658-1
eBook ISBN: 1-59540-758-8

Purchase *"The Man From The Clouds"*
as a traditional bound book at:
www.1stWorldLibrary.org/purchase.asp?ISBN=1-59540-658-1

The Man From The Clouds
contributed by the Charles Family
in support of
1st World Library Literary Society

CONTENTS

PART I

PART II

PART I

I

IN THE CLOUDS

"My God," said Rutherford, "the cable has broken!"

In an instant I was craning over the side of the basket. Five hundred feet, 700 feet, 1000 feet, 2000 feet below us, the cruiser that had been our only link with the world of man was diminishing so swiftly that, as far as I remember, she had shrunk to the smallness of a tug and then vanished into the haze before I even answered him.

"Anything to be done?" I asked.

"Nothing," said he.

It had been growing steadily more misty even down near the water, and now as the released balloon shot up into an altitude of five, ten, and presently twelve thousand feet, everything in Heaven and earth disappeared except that white and clammy fog. By a simultaneous impulse he lit a cigarette and I a pipe, and I remember very plainly wondering whether he felt any touch of that self-conscious defiance of fate and deliberate intention to do the coolest thing possible, which I am free to confess I felt myself. Probably not; Rutherford was the real Navy and I but a zig-zag ringed R.N.V.R. amateur. Still, the spirit of the Navy is infectious and I made a fair attempt to keep his stout heart company.

"What *ought* to happen to a thing like this?" I enquired.

"If this wind holds we might conceivably make a landing somewhere - with extraordinary luck."

"On the other side?"

He nodded and I reflected.

It was towards the end of August, 1914. We were somewhere about the middle of the North Sea when the observation balloon was sent up, and I had persuaded Rutherford to take me up with him in the basket. Five minutes ago I had been telling myself I was the luckiest R.N.V.R. Sub-Lieutenant in the Navy; and then suddenly the appalling thing happened. I may not give away any naval secrets, but everybody knows, I presume, that towed balloons are sometimes used at sea, and it is pretty obvious that certain accidents are liable to happen to them. In this case the most obvious of all accidents happened; the cable snapped, and there we were heading, as far as I could judge, for the stars that twinkle over the German coast. At least, our aneroid showed that we were going upwards faster than any bird could rise, and the west wind was blowing straight for the mouth of the Elbe when we last felt it - for, of course, in a free balloon one ceases to feel wind altogether.

Neither of us spoke for some time, and then a thought struck me suddenly and I asked: -

"Did you notice what o'clock it was when we broke loose?"

Rutherford nodded.

"I'm taking the time," said he, "and assuming the twenty knot breeze holds, we might risk a drop about six o'clock."

"A drop" meant jumping into space and trusting one's parachute to do its business properly. I felt a sudden tightening inside me as I thought of that dive into the void, but I asked calmly enough:

"And assuming the breeze doesn't hold?"

"Oh, it will hold all right; it will rise if anything," said he.

We had only been shipmates for a week (that being the extent of my nautical experience), but I had learned enough about Rutherford in that time to know that he was one of the most positive and self-confident men breathing. One had to make allowance for this; still, that is the kind of company one wants in an involuntary balloon expedition across the North Sea through a dense fog.

"And where are we likely to come down?" I enquired.

"We might make the German coast as far south as Borkum or one of the other islands, or we might land somewhere as far north as Holstein."

"Not Holland or Denmark?"

He shook his head positively, "No such luck."

Though this was a trifle depressing, it was comforting to feel that one was with a man who knew his way about the air so thoroughly. I looked at our map, judged the wind, and decided that he was probably right. The chances of fetching a neutral country seemed very slender. Curiously enough the chances of never reaching any country at all had passed out of my calculations for the moment. Rutherford was so perfectly assured.

"And what's the programme when we do land?" I asked.

"Well, we've got to get out of the place as quickly as possible. That's pretty evident."

"How?"

"You know the lingo, don't you?"

"Pretty well."

"Well enough not to be spotted as a foreigner?"

"I almost think so."

"First thing I ever heard to the credit of the diplomatic service!" he laughed. "Well, you'll have to pitch a yarn of some kind if we fall in with any of the natives. Of course we'll try and avoid 'em if we can, and work across country either for Denmark or Holland by compass."

"Have you got a compass?" I asked.

"Damn!" he exclaimed, and for a few moments a frown settled on his bull dog face. Then it cleared again and he said, "After all we'll have to move about by night and the stars will do just as well."

He was never much of a talker and after this he fell absolutely silent and I was left to my thoughts. Though I had fortunately put on plenty of extra clothes for the ascent, I began to feel chilly up at that altitude enshrouded in that cold white mist, and I don't mind admitting that my thoughts gradually became a little more serious than (to be quite honest) they usually are. I hardly think Rutherford, with all his virtues, had much imagination. I have a good deal - a little too much at times - and several other possible endings to our voyage besides a safe landing and triumphant escape began to present themselves. Two especially I had to steel my thoughts against continually - a descent with a parachute that declined to open, whether on to German or any other soil, or else a splash and then a brief struggle in the cold North Sea. I am no great swimmer and it would be soon over.

And so the hours slowly passed; always the same mist and generally the same silence. Occasionally we talked a little, and then for a long space our voices would cease and there would be utter and absolute quiet, - not the smallest sound of any sort or kind. We had been silent for a long, long time and I had done quite as much thinking as was good for my nerves, when Rutherford suddenly exclaimed,

"We are over land!"

He was looking over the edge of the basket, and instantly I was staring into space on my side. There was certainly nothing to see but mist.

"I can smell land," said he, "and I heard something just now."

"At this height!" I exclaimed.

"We are down to well under six thousand feet," said he.

I wanted to be convinced, but this was more than I could believe.

"The smell must be devilish strong," I observed. "And I'm afraid I must have a cold in my head. Besides, it's only five-thirty."

As I have said, poor Rutherford was the most positive fellow in the world. He stuck to it that we were over land, but I managed to persuade him to wait a little longer to make sure. He waited half an hour and when he spoke then I could see that his mind was made up.

"We are falling pretty rapidly," said he, "and personally I'd sooner take my chance in a parachute than stick in this basket till we bump. If one is going to try a drop, the great thing is to see that it's a long drop. Parachutes don't always open as quick as they're intended to. At any moment we may begin to fall suddenly, so I'm going overboard now."

My own career has hitherto failed to convince my friends that prudence is my besetting virtue, but whether it was the sobering effect of those long hours of chilly thinking, or whether my good angel came to my rescue, I know not; anyhow I shook my head as firmly as he nodded his.

"We have only been going the minimum time you allowed for making land," I argued, "and quite possibly the breeze may have dropped a bit. Honestly I haven't heard a sound or smelt a smell that faintly suggested land underneath, and we can still drop a lot more and have room to take to the parachutes. Let's wait till we get down to one thousand feet."

"You do as you please," said he. "I'm going over."

"And I'm not going yet," said I.

We looked at one another in silence for a moment, and then he held out his hand.

"Well, good-bye and good luck!" said he.

"Wait a little bit longer!" I implored him.

"My dear Merton," he said, "I feel it in my bones that we've been going a lot faster than we calculated. In fact I *know* we have! One gets an instinct for that sort of thing, and also one gets a sort of general idea when to cut the basket and jump. I tell you we've been over land for the last half hour. Come on, old chap, I honestly advise you to jump too."

I almost yielded, but some instinct seemed to hold me back. The thought that he might think I was deserting him, the suspicion that he suspected I was a little afraid of the drop, nearly drove me over the edge of the basket with him. I felt a brute for hanging back, but in my heart I felt just as certain he was jumping too soon as he felt that I was waiting too long. So I shook his hand, and over he went; I had one glimpse of something dark below me, and then the mist swallowed him up. Rutherford was gone, and I may as well say now that not a sign of him was ever seen again.

If you want to know what loneliness - real horrifying loneliness - is like, I know no better recipe than drifting through a fog in a balloon, with your only companion gone, and not the faintest belief in your heart that you are within a hundred miles of any square inch of earth. I almost think the fact that the balloon was steadily sinking and that sooner or later I should have to leap from it too was the one thing that kept my spirits anyways up to the mark. The prospect of even the most desperate action was better than interminably facing that clammy void.

Though the chance of making land seemed to me infinitesimally remote by this time, yet in case I had such almost inconceivable luck, it was well to make some preparations for having a run for my money in an enemy country. I took off my uniform coat, transferring everything I wanted to keep from its pockets to those of my oilskin. I then put this on and buttoned it up, and of course I took off my cap.

And then I smoked another pipe and watched the aneroid and tried not to think at all, till with a start I realised we were considerably less than a thousand feet above - the land or the sea? Heaven knew which, but we were falling fast and there was no more time to lose. I hitched the parachute on to my leg, got on the edge of the basket, and then - well, I all but funked it. I remember my last thought was a horrible simile of a man jumping off a tree with a rope round his neck, and then somehow or other I forced myself to let go.

Concerning the next few seconds I can give no statistics, whether as to height or pace. I only know that when I first became conscious of anything, I was drifting like a snow flake down through the mist, and that I could fill several pages with my thoughts in the course of that drift. It seemed to me that there was hardly an incident in my life which didn't fly through my brain like a cinema being worked at lightning speed. Some of the most vivid incidents were the last three balls of the over in which I topped the century in the 'Varsity match, my interview with my poor dear uncle when I broke the news that I had to face the official receiver and chuck the diplomatic service, and the first night of "Bill's All Right" when I made my début on the stage. A brilliant career! And very swiftly reviewed, for just as I had reached the theatrical episodes, there was an extraordinary change in the light, and my thoughts very abruptly shifted from my past misdemeanours.

It had been evening when I dropped from the clouds, but the mist kept the light very white though rather dim. Now a sudden blackness seemed to rise up underneath my descending feet, and at the same moment the mist thinned out till I could see for a space all round below me. This space was green and almost before I realised what the greenness meant I was sitting in a field of clover.

II

THE MAN ON THE SHORE

The breeze that had been driving the balloon along high overhead was evidently an upper current only, for it was almost quite still in that clover field. What between the falling of evening and the thin mist, my vision was limited to a radius of about a quarter of a mile or so, but I can assure you I studied that visible space more intently than I have ever studied anything in my life. It seemed to be an almost flat country I had landed in, all cultivated but very bare. I was within fifty yards or so of a low rough stone wall, and on the further side of that lay a field of corn. On every other side other fields faded into the evening and the mist, and that was all there was to be seen. I saw no sign of a house, or of a tree, or of a hedgerow, and I heard not a sound but the cry of a distant sea bird.

In the gay days when I was attaché at Berlin I had acquired a fair general acquaintance with Germany, and I instantly put down the place I had landed in as some part of the flat wind-swept country not far from the North Sea coast. In fact the crying seagull suggested that the shore was fairly close at hand. This so exactly fitted in with our calculations that I made up my mind definitely and at once to start with it as a working hypothesis and behave accordingly.

But how precisely was one to behave accordingly? In which direction should I turn? What should I aim at? Should I look for a house or a native and trust to my German still being up to its old high water mark, or should I lie low for the night? I simply stood and wondered for some minutes, and then I decided on one prompt and immediate deed. The parachute must be hidden, so far as that countryside was capable of hiding anything.

I packed it up as neatly as I could, and then started for the low wall. My first steps on the firm ground with its soft mat of clover and grasses gave me an extraordinary sensation of pleasure. Merely to be alive and on the earth again seemed to leave nothing to wish for. Close to the wall a peewee rose suddenly from my feet and flapped off into the dusk with one melancholy cry after another. "Peewee! Peewee!" I shall never hear that sound without thinking of that lonesome misty field. I stopped and looked round me anxiously, but not a living thing besides had been disturbed, and presently I was stowing the parachute away in a bed of high rank grass and docken just under the wall.

Then I stood still and listened again. Once more a distant sea bird cried and I decided to make for the sound on the chance of finding the coast line and getting at least one bearing. I followed the line of the wall, crossed another low wall and another field of thin rough grass, and then I realised that I was almost on the brink of the sea. The wash of the swell on rocks met my ear and the dull misty green of the land faded into the misty grey of wide waters.

I stepped over yet another of those low tumbledown walls and now I was on the crisp short grass that fringes coasts, with rocks before me and the sea quite visible about thirty feet below. So I had just made land and no more ! Poor Rutherford ; I guessed his fate at once.

A little aimlessly I set out to the left. Somehow or other I had got it into my head that I was nearer the Dutch than the Danish border and my idea was to head for a neutral country. The coast line swung inland round a cove and at the same time dipped sharply, and hardly had I turned to follow it when a figure seemed to spring up out of the dip.

Whether the man had been squatting down, or whether it was the slope of the ground that suddenly revealed him, I know not, but there he was not ten paces away. I could see that he wore an oilskin and sou'wester and judged him at once as a fisherman.

"Good evening!" I cried genially in my best German. "It's a fine night!"

"Good evening!" said he, also in German and quite involuntarily it seemed, for the next instant he spoke again in a very different key, and *in English.*

"My God! Are you insane?" he said in a low intense voice and with a distinct trace of guttural accent. "Don't speak German here! Have you no other language? Don't you speak English?"

I don't know whether you could have literally knocked me down with a feather, but a stout feather would certainly have come pretty near doing it. I simply gaped at him.

Again he spoke; this time in German, but almost in a whisper.

"Do not speak German here so loudly! Do you not know any English?"

A dim perception of the almost incredible truth began to dawn on me and I did my best to grapple with the situation. I had to account for my astonished stare; that was the first thought that flashed through my head.

"Of course I speak English," I said, and by the favour of Heaven I found myself instinctively saying those words in the very accents of the German waiter in "Bill's All Right" (my first offence on the professional stage), "but I thought you were Hans Eckstein. I could hardly believe my own eyes!"

"Hans Eckstein? Who is he?" demanded my new acquaintance, and I was pleased to observe no suspicion in his voice, merely a little astonishment.

"A friend," I answered glibly, "one of us."

He looked at me for a moment, very narrowly, and in those seconds of silence I began to realise more exactly what must have happened. The upper current of air had been blowing *westwards* - not eastwards as the wind blew on the surface. The good land under my feet was assuredly not Germany; almost certainly it must be part of my own blessed native island, or why this insistence on my speaking English, rather than, say, Dutch or Danish? And then the man I was speaking to, what must he obviously be? There was only one answer possible.

I may add that I had the presence of mind not to stare blankly at him while I thought these thoughts. I let him do the staring while I fished my pipe out of my oilskin pocket and began to fill it.

"So!" he murmured, and I thought he seemed satisfied enough, especially as he asked with manifest curiosity but without any apparent suspicion in his voice, "And how did you get here?"

Yet when I looked up from my pipe-filling to answer him I could almost swear that he had done something to make his features less visible - pulled his sou'wester further down and sunk his chin into the high collar of his oilskin, it certainly seemed to me. As I had gathered a very insufficient impression of him before, this was a little provoking. Still, I told myself that our acquaintance was only beginning. How to ripen it - that was the problem. I tried the effect of merely winking and saying with a cool, knowing air:

"The usual way. Do you have to ask?"

He looked sharply up and down the rocks and out to sea and I saw instantly what was in his mind.

"Impossible! There was no signal. I have been looking out all the time," said he.

I merely laughed.

"How else do you think I could have come?"

"So!" he murmured again, and then he asked a curious question.

"Do you know if there are many sheep on this island?"

So I had landed on an island! That was the first and chief deduction I drew from this enquiry. The second was that the man's English must be a little weak. Obviously he meant something rather different from what he said.

"Sheep?" I said with a laugh. "No, my friend, I have something else to do than count sheep."

Again he looked at me for a moment, his face now almost completely hidden by the peak of his sou'wester. If by any chance he were still doubting me the best thing seemed to be a touch of candour and an appeal he could scarcely resist.

"See here," I said, lowering my voice, "I want to stop in this island to-night. In fact those are my orders. Now where can you find me a safe place?"

He lowered his voice too. In fact he seemed to reciprocate my confidence very satisfactorily.

"We must be very careful. I must see that the coast is clear first. Just you sit and wait here for ten minutes. I will be back."

He nodded at me to enforce his injunctions and added as he turned away,

"Keep sitting down. Mind that!"

I sat down, finished filling my pipe, lit it, and waited. And as I waited I frankly confess I fairly hugged myself. Never before was there such a bit of luck, thought I. That that vagabond balloon should actually bring its passenger back to his native land instead of dropping him in the sea or landing him in Germany was fortunate almost beyond belief, but that he should then stumble on a German spy and actually convince the man that he was a confederate and lead him straight into the net already spreading for him, surely showed that after a considerable run of ill luck (and, I must confess, ill guidance), the passenger had suddenly become Fortune's prime favourite. Several very eligible and commodious castles were constructed in the night air by that lonely shore as I sat and smoked.

And then I heard a cautious but distinct whistle, and up I jumped and looked all round me. There was no one to be seen, but the sound came from the right - the way I had come, and I set off through the thickening dusk in that direction. But the odd thing was that I walked considerably further than the sound of the whistle could have carried and never a sign of human being or of house did I see - nothing but that desolate grassy sea-board and the faintly gleaming waters.

I stopped and began to wonder, and then I heard the whistle again. It was still ahead of me, so on I walked and once more the same thing occurred. This time I paused for at least another ten minutes, but nobody appeared and nothing whatever happened. There I was, utterly alone once more, with the land growing black and the sea dim and not a sound now even from the sea gulls.

J. Storer Clouston

III

ALONE AGAIN

"The man has suspected me!" I said to myself.

It was an unpleasant conclusion, but the more carefully I thought over every little circumstance the more certain I felt it was the true one. To begin with, there was the way in which he kept his face concealed after the first few sentences we exchanged. Then there was that curious question about the sheep. It must have been a password - I saw that now, and I could have kicked myself for not seeing it sooner. Of course I had no idea of the proper answer, but I might at least have replied with some equally cryptic sentence and tried to bluff him into thinking I was using a different code. As it was, I had made it perfectly obvious that I had missed the point absolutely.

Finally there was his conduct in slipping away and leaving me stranded like this. Surely it was the very last trick to play on an accomplice. In fact it settled the matter. But why then did he whistle - and, moreover, whistle twice?

For a few minutes I was utterly puzzled, and then an explanation flashed upon me. He wished to lead me in this particular direction! And why? Evidently because he himself was living or hiding in the other. I tried to put myself in his shoes and think what I would do myself, and if I had had the wit to think of it, that would obviously be the soundest thing. So obvious did it seem to me that I decided to set to work on that assumption.

First of all I walked a little further to see if I could test this theory, and in a minute or two I saw dimly ahead of me houses near the beach. I stopped and thought again. Could it possibly be that this was the refuge he was providing and that he did not suspect me after all?

"In that case," I said to myself, "would any man in his senses use such a vague and misleading method of conducting a friend, especially when a mistake might be - and probably would be - fatal to his schemes? Obviously not!"

On the other hand, these houses fitted excellently into the theory that he wanted me to take shelter there simply because they were well removed from his own lair.

"And then what's the fellow doing himself all this time?" I thought. "Evidently scuttling back in the opposite direction!"

So back I turned and set out on a very cheerless and solitary walk. There was no sense of immediate action ahead now, no anticipation of any further excitement this night, and, the more I came to think of it, not one chance in a thousand of stumbling upon the man again even though I were really heading towards him.

As I walked along that dark shore, I tried to think out

all the possibilities of the situation.

"Is the man living on this island?" (assuming it is an island, and as the sheep weren't real sheep it may not be a real island) I asked myself. "Or has he simply landed from a submarine or some other enemy craft, and by this time is hurrying off again?"

I recalled our conversation, especially his words when I said I had arrived in "the usual way." "Impossible! There was no signal. I have been looking out all the time," he had answered. Surely that implied he was living here on shore, and indeed his very presence alone by himself and his whole attitude and behaviour were consistent only with that theory.

"What conclusions has he come to about me?" was my next question, and as I debated this problem my spirits began to rise a little.

"Hang it, he must be puzzled!" I said to myself confidently, and I do think justly. "For supposing I were on his job in Germany and an entire stranger suddenly sprang up out of nowhere, hailed me in excellent English, and then (even if he didn't know the particular riddle I used as pass-word) conducted himself like a confederate, made no attempt to arrest me or interfere with me, and spoke German with a distinct English accent, what would I think?"

I debated the answer for some minutes and then it came to me involuntarily and inevitably.

"I'd be dashed if I'd know what to think! And that's just exactly the hole this fellow must be in. I may be a fellow Hun and I may be an enemy, and he has got to make up his mind which. So far I'm quite certain he hasn't enough evidence either way."

The obvious corollary to this was that he must be presented with evidence which would make him think me a fellow Hun. Of course this assumed that he would have some means of getting news of my doings and my movements and forming conclusions from what he heard. But I thought it a pretty safe assumption to make. Confederates the man must have, and he would certainly tell them of the mysterious stranger, and the whole gang as certainly would make it their business to learn everything about me.

"What would a fellow Hun do in my place?" I said to myself. "Knowing the breed as I do, he would certainly overdo the patriotic John Bull business, he would be a little too polite to everybody, and he would eat like a hog."

This then should be my role, and I may as well confess honestly that the last item appealed to me particularly. I kept on smoking till my head reeled in the hope of forgetting my hunger, but between pipes I felt ready to chew my oilskin. Of course I should also keep up a touch of the German waiter accent, and if this programme failed to lead either to my arrest or to my friend coming to my rescue, I felt that my reputation both as an ex-diplomatist and a rising young actor would be seriously tarnished.

And then all at once a light seemed to be extinguished in my brain. I ceased to be able to think any longer and my knees felt shaky as I walked. It was the reaction after what had really been a pretty long strain of one kind and another. Looking back, it seems now inevitable enough, but at the time I felt desperately ashamed of myself. Perhaps I might have been able to pull myself together had I chanced to fall in with that oilskinned figure again, but I thought at the moment I had become utterly useless and I felt inclined to throw myself down on the grass and go to sleep and forget everything. In fact I very soon should have, when I saw at last some farm buildings close ahead. They stood on the edge of a small cove and the ground dipped down to them so that they were not against the sky line, and I had nearly walked straight into the wall of an out-house before I saw a sign of them.

And then I remember rather hazily knocking at a door and presently finding myself in a low kitchen with a peat fire burning on an open hearth and what seemed to be dozens of people sitting round it. I probably counted each of them three or four times over.

They gave me a huge bowl of milk and a pile of oat cakes and cheese, and the one item of my programme I carried out faithfully was to eat like a famished animal. I believe I put some sort of an accent into the few words I murmured, but most of the time my mouth was too full for much conversation. I know that I never attempted any explanation of how I got there, and that night nobody asked me, and I certainly postponed the patriotic John Bull business.

When I finished my supper I felt better, but still a little dazed. There now seemed to be fewer in the family, but my eyes must still have been multiplying them for I thought there were three or four rather pretty girls, presumably daughters, with high pink cheeks, when there actually turned out next morning to be only two; and two poor idiots, presumably sons, with unpleasant stares and stubbly beards and open mouths, when daylight revealed only one. In fact the father of the household and his wife were the only people I counted accurately.

And then I remember being led to the barn, and seeing a vast pile of soft hay and throwing myself into the midst of it; and there my recollections of that day end. I actually had not even enquired into what part of the world I had dropped.

IV

THE SUSPICIOUS STRANGER

There seem to be two distinct kinds of dreamers; to judge at least from their confessions next morning. There is the superior kind which dreams a condensed novel and remembers it distinctly to retail at breakfast, and there is the inferior kind which only carries away a vague impression of having vaguely striven to stride out and escape from some nebulous horror, or of trying to purchase a pound of golf balls at a counter which would persist in turning into a couple of parallel bars or a roll-top writing desk. Personally I belong to the inferior species, and I cannot even swear that I really had a dream at all that night. I only know that when I woke up at last I found that my oilskin was unbuttoned and thrown back, whereas I thought I had gone to sleep with it buttoned up; and that when I noticed this, I then began to have a confused memory of a dream wherein I was seized by some one or something and struggled violently to free myself.

I sat up in my bed of straw and looked round me. The sunshine was streaming through a small window and under the door, but the door was closed, the bar was very still and quite empty save for my own presence, and the crowing of a cock and the clucking of hens were at first the only sounds that reached me from outside. Then I became conscious of a soft and regular "swish," rising and falling constantly and perpetually, and I remembered the sea close at hand, and a shiver of gratitude ran through me to think how narrowly I had escaped having that heaving surface fathoms over my head.

I have often wished since that I had lain there for a little while and tried to remember the dream, and whether I had actually gone to sleep with my oilskin buttoned, while the circumstances, such as they were, were fresh in my memory. When I thought of them afterwards I could swear to nothing and finally concluded the whole thing was probably fancy.

But if by any chance it were not, then evidently *some one* had tried to search me in the night, and who would it be likely to be but my vanished acquaintance on the shore, or his confederates? And in that case one of them must have been lurking very close at hand. However, when I tried to piece my recollections together afterwards it was too late to make anything of them at all.

I only know for certain that I missed nothing from my pockets, and that as a matter of fact I had actually carried nothing in them that would have given me away - so far at least as I could judge.

These, as I say, were my subsequent reflections. What I did at the time was not to think about the matter any further, but jump up, open the barn door and walk out into the sunshine. It was now about ten o'clock on a flawless August morning, and not easily shall I forget the picture of that blue sea gently heaving far out to a bright horizon, and the semi-circle of white sand fringing the little cove, and the glimpse of green and smiling inland country, and the group of low grey farm buildings just out of reach of the wash of the waves. Whatever part of the world it might be, I felt entirely satisfied with it.

I stood for a few minutes gazing absently out to sea, and rehearsing in my mind my plan of campaign. My voice, manners and conduct must be such that if by some stroke of luck I actually fell in with my friend of last night or one of his confederates they would assume I was a friend and at least give me a nod, wink, password, or something to test me - and I vowed I would overlook nothing suspicious this time.

If, however, as was unfortunately far more likely, I met mere honest folk, they would quickly spread the news that a suspicious stranger was in the neighbourhood, and surely the report would reach at least one of the gang (for I confidently assumed a gang), and they would make it their business to seek me out. Finally I decided I had no time to waste, for several reasons. Through the clucking hens I strolled across to the dwelling house and there in the kitchen I found the mother, one of the pink-cheeked daughters, and the idiot son. They set about getting me some breakfast, and a few minutes later in came the father and another son, a strapping fellow not in the least resembling the idiot, and shortly afterwards appeared the other daughter.

I gave them my proper name, Roger Merton, since it was just the sort of ultra English name which a disguised Hun would adopt, and I learned that theirs was Scollay: - Peter Scollay, the father, Mrs. Scollay, Peter, the younger, Maggie, and Jane; besides Jock, the idiot. I was excessively affable, and they were not openly cool, but I noticed with satisfaction that they were far from demonstrative, with the marked exception of Jock who burst into several very loud and friendly laughs on extremely small provocation. He was horrid to look at, but I could not help feeling rather friendly towards the only member of the household who exhibited a glimpse of geniality, even though I was doing my level best to chill them.

As for the others, Peter Scollay the senior was a big tawny-bearded fellow, undeniably handsome despite one small defect. His eyes were a trifle too hard and cautious, and in one of them was a distinct cast. Curiously enough, his wife also had a slight cast, and so it was not surprising to see a trace of this in Peter junior and his red-cheeked sisters. Jock, however, seemed to have been endowed with imbecility instead of a cast. Apart from him, they were all good-looking, despite the family defect; and they were all very reticent this morning. I seemed indeed to trace the father's wariness as well as the cast in each pair of eyes that furtively studied me.

"And your very beautiful island," I enquired, in guttural accents that would have made me flee for the police instantly, had I been in their shoes, "so pleasantly situated in the sea - what is its name?"

They looked a little astonished, as well they might, and then in dry accents the father replied, "Ransay."

"Ransay?" I repeated, and then all at once I realised where I was. Ransay was one of the northern isles of that not unknown archipelago which at the present moment it is safer to leave unnamed. Or perhaps for purposes of reference one may call it The Windy Isles. Somewhere in the same archipelago, twenty or thirty miles to the south'ard, was a particularly important naval base and I began to realise what I had stumbled up against.

In those early days of the war one heard a great many tales of spies and spying, but many of them were so palpably absurd and there was as yet such a total lack of evidence to support any one of them, that I - like a good many other people - felt sceptical of the whole thing. The distinguished General in German pay, the well known member of the Cabinet in hourly communication with the Kaiser, the group of German strategists working in the cellars of a West End London mansion, and all the rest of the early legends had made even the very moderately sensible extremely chary of believing anything we heard. But I thought very hard and seriously now. A real spy - seen and heard - actually living in the Isle of Ransay, in the back premises, so to speak, of that all important base, with Heaven only knew what means of the information concerning matters to the south'ard, and in immediate touch with any marauders who might tap gently at the back door on a dark night; here was something to sober even a bankrupt ex-light-comedian.

I kept my mouth very full while I thought these thoughts and conscientiously made the typical German chewing noise, and by the time my lips were cleared for action again a beaming smile enwreathed them.

"Do you have many ships which pass this way?" I enquired.

The question was a great success. Jock laughed with

vacant glee and the rest of the family exchanged glances.

"No' very many," said Mr. Scollay warily.

Now I decided to give them the John Bull turn.

"No German ships I am sure!" I cried through a mouthful of porridge. "They are cowards! They will not venture *here* - no fears! They fear our brave sailors too much! Aha! We know that, eh?"

They agreed as coldly as I could wish. Evidently I was producing a thoroughly bad impression. At the same time nobody broke into whispered German, or made any comment that could conceivably be taken for a pass-word. I thought I would try giving them one myself.

"Are there many sheep in this island?" I asked.

Jock emitted another blast of genial laughter and Mr. Scollay as cautiously as ever replied,

"A good few."

But there was no sign of any secret understanding of my words, and reluctantly I began to come to the conclusion that neither my friend of last night nor any of his confederates were here. It is true that the position of the house fitted my theory, and that its lonely situation on the very edge of the sea was ideal, and quite possibly these people might know more than they ought, they might in fact be abettors of treason and concealers of traitors, but that they were not the principals seemed evident enough.

Still, in any event it seemed to me of prime importance to disseminate a report of a suspicious stranger as widely and quickly as possible, so I selected the middle of another mouthful as the moment of enquiring.

"This pretty farm, my friend, does it belong to you?"

"No," said my host, "the island a' belongs to Mr. Rendall."

" So ! " said I. " And this Mr. Rendall, where does he live - in London?"

"Not him!" said Mr. Scollay, "he bides in Ransay."

I pricked up my ears at this, and my spy-hunt seemed suddenly a much more promising venture. Some of the difficulties of playing a lone hand had already become apparent. But with some one I could confide in, some one who would know everybody in the island and a good deal about them, and who could advise and abet me, it seemed heavy odds against my vanished friend evading me for long.

"I think perhaps I ought to pay my respects to Mr. Rendall," I said in a doubtful ruminating way, as though I were debating whether it were quite a safe move.

"You'll find him at home," was all the comment my host made.

But now that there was a prospect of losing their suspicious visitor, the family all at once set about extracting some information regarding the manner of his arrival in their midst.

"You'll no have been long in Ransay?" began my hostess.

"Oh no, just a short time," I beamed.

"You'll not have come by the boat," pronounced my host.

"Not *the* boat, but surely I must have come by *a* boat!" I smiled. "I cannot swim from Aberdeen!"

I don't know exactly why I mentioned Aberdeen, but it seemed to have a distinctly sedative effect.

"You'll not be a dealer?" enquired my host.

Here was a simple solution thrust into my hand. For a moment I thought of confessing I actually was a dealer and had got too drunk last night to remember how I arrived. But then I feared the tale might sound too credible and the reports of a suspicious stranger be stifled at their birth.

"Well," I said, "I do deal in some things."

I could see that suspicion had revived and I thought it better to leave it at that, and be off. With a little difficulty I made my hosts take payment for my night's lodging, and then asked for directions to the laird's mansion.

"You'll no can miss it," said Mr. Scollay.

" It's the big house. Just keep along the road and you'll

see it afore you."

So off I set through this unknown isle, still hatless and buttoned up in my oilskin, but smoking a peculiarly soothing pipe and thoroughly enjoying my adventure. The prospect of an ally ahead was delightfully cheering.

"Provided Mr. Rendall isn't an utter ass, we ought to have these fellows sitting!" I said to myself.

V

THE DOCTOR'S HOUSE

The rough road from the shore kept gently mounting and I soon stood high enough to get a very good general idea of the island of Ransay. It was a green, low-lying, undulating fragment of the world, set that morning in a sea of sapphire blue, open to the horizon on the one hand and strewn with sister isles on the other. The Scollay's house stood near the northwest end, and beyond it there seemed to be little save sea-turf and rocks, but in the direction I was walking one small green farm followed another for what I guessed to be four or five miles, and from side to side perhaps a couple of miles or less. There was only one rise in the land that could be called a hill, and that only by courtesy; elsewhere nothing but green undulations with a small reedy loch or two tucked away in their gentle folds.

Far to the southward, on other isles, higher hills, brown and blue, broke the horizon, but apart from these one saw nothing but a green and blue plain lying beneath an immensity of white and blue sky. With sea birds hovering and crying and larks mounting and singing over this, and the sun shining, and a northwest breeze that tasted like dry champagne, and myriads of wild flowers, yellow, blue, white, red, pink, and purple, underfoot, I felt almost too light-hearted. In fact I actually started singing, and only stopped when I bethought me that it was a trifle inconsistent with the character of a man slinking about in fear of his life, looking for a fellow miscreant to befriend him.

But it was quite impossible not to feel elated. Now that I realised the limited size of the place and its open surface, it was obvious that no man could lurk there unknown to the inhabitants. He must live in a house and pass for one of themselves. It seemed then impossible to believe (especially with an ally in prospect) that a spy whom I had actually seen and talked with (and knew moreover to have a foreign accent) could escape my clutches. And, apart from patriotic motives, of what a lift that would give to my tarnished character!

"Let me recall the fellow carefully," said I to myself, "and get his face and voice well into my head against our next meeting."

I tried to reconstruct our first meeting exactly as it had happened, to see again that dark figure rise in my path, and look into the face beneath the sou'wester. I shall not say precisely that this endeavour shook my confidence, but it certainly made me realise that I should have to set to work very warily to trap the man, for the harder I tried to see in my mind's eye that face distinctly, the less distinct it grew. I could certainly swear to a moustache, and I felt pretty sure there was a beard as well, but not absolutely certain. He was of middle height, say between 5 feet 6, and 5 feet 10; but that was a fairly wide margin. In fact all I could positively swear to was that he was neither an obviously tall nor an obviously short man.

As to his build, he seemed thick-set and sturdy, but then who does not in an oilskin coat? It would take a very slight figure indeed to look slender in an oilskin. So here again I could only say that he was neither a remarkably stout man nor a remarkably thin man. And this was really all I could swear to in the matter of his outward appearance; though I told myself confidently enough that if I actually fell in with him again I should recognise him fast enough.

"He can't disguise his voice anyhow," I said to myself.

And then here again I began to realise a small difficulty; though nothing, it seemed to me very serious. After his first involuntary reply to me in German, the man had spoken in low, half-whispered tones. In ordinary conversation, especially if he were on his guard, he would speak quite differently. But could he eradicate his distinct touch of foreign accent? No; I thought decidedly that was beyond him.

I was so immersed in my thoughts that I had become quite oblivious to everything outside them. Beyond the fact that I had struck a hard macadamed road and was striding down it, I realised nothing else, till of a sudden I looked up and noticed a large house close before me, and at that I stopped dead and awoke from my reverie.

That it was Mr. Rendall's mansion I never doubted. I saw now that it was not a really big house, but it was large compared with the small farm houses, and its utterly bare situation and the way in which it was set on a slight rise in the ground made it seem obviously the "big hoose" I was looking for. But somehow or other at the sight of it my spirits were instantly damped. Indeed I never saw a chillier, less inviting looking habitation, or one that seemed to repel confidence in it more subtly.

The road ran straight at it and then curved round the low wall that bounded the domains. And these domains consisted of absolutely nothing more than a rough grass paddock with a short straight drive leading from an open and dilapidated iron gate in the wall just where the curve began. There was no ivy, or any sort of creeper on the walls, but, instead, a sort of grey-green damp hue, broken only by a very few staring windows. I passed through that dilapidated gate with no temptation at all to sing.

The drive was covered with an infamous species of large pebble, so uncomfortable to walk on that I chose the grass at the side and I only stepped on to this apology for gravel when I was quite close to the house; approaching the front of it, I may say, at an angle. My footsteps made a noise like a cart and horse, and instantly down went the blind of the nearest window of the ground floor.

I stopped dead instinctively and looked at this bleak mansion narrowly. At the angle from which I had approached the front, I could see the blind go down quite plainly, but it was impossible to get even a glimpse into the room behind it.

"What the devil!" I murmured.

And then I told myself that I was really getting too suspicious. It must be a lady's bed-room obviously. The ground floor near the front door seemed an odd place for such an apartment. Still, one never knows what a lady's fancy may be. In any case there was nothing to be achieved by standing there staring, so I resumed my resounding progress across the pebbles.

I was at the front door and just going to ring, when round the corner of the house, right ahead of me, appeared a gentleman, and my spirits fell still further. I can't exactly say that his was a face I disliked, but it was decidedly not one I took to. He had eyes set somewhat close together, a well trimmed short black beard, and an expression in which I seemed to read impudence and certainly read suspicion. He stopped at the sight of me and looked me up and down at least as curiously as I studied him. Only I trust I conducted my inspection less obviously.

"Mr. Rendall?" I enquired, and though I had come here meaning to confide in him, I found myself instinctively putting in a touch of accent; not with a wet brush as I did for the Scollays' benefit, still I threw in a little, and, as I say, quite without intending it.

Curiously enough I saw his face clear the moment I spoke.

"Oh," said he, with an air of relief, "it's the doctor you're wanting, is it? Well, he's at home. Come in."

So the laird was a doctor? Of which sort, I wondered; medical, theological, or what?

"I'm Mr. O'Brien," added my new acquaintance as he opened the front door for me. "You're quite sure it's not me you're wanting?"

I had noticed more than a trace of accent in his own voice when he spoke, and there was no doubt now what it was; a very palpable Irish brogue. As he asked this question he looked at me with a curious mixture of humour and defiance. It seemed to me that the humour was assumed and the defiance genuine, but that may have been simply because the man impressed me unfavourably.

"No," I replied with a continental bow, "I am not so fortunate."

And then suddenly a thought flashed across me. Ought I to have answered in a very different key? But we were in the hall now and the next moment another gentleman appeared.

"Here's Dr. Rendall," said Mr. O'Brien, and I bowed again.

"My name is Mr. Roger Merton," I explained. "I have taken the liberty of calling upon you."

"Come into my study, Mr. Merton," said Dr. Rendall.

He spoke in a friendly enough voice, but if there was not a trace of suspicion in his eye too, I am greatly mistaken. And in both cases it seemed to me that it was suspicion tinged with apprehension, rather than the suspicion I was so deliberately cultivating. Indeed, I had not intended to cultivate any suspicion at all in this house, but fortunately (I think) I simply acted automatically.

Taking him altogether, Dr. Rendall was a decidedly more prepossessing looking man than O'Brien. In fact he was rather good-looking, with grey hair and moustache, face of a deep bronze-red hue and very blue eyes. He was well set up, and quite well dressed too in rough tweeds, and the only thing against him was that look in his eye as we exchanged our first sentences.

My wits were very wide awake by this time; I carried a picture of the outside of the house distinctly in my head as we turned out of the hall, and when we entered the study I knew it for the room where the blind had shut down.

"Is Mrs. Rendall at home?" I enquired.

O'Brien laughed.

"There are no ladies in this house, but just the doctor and me!" said he.

So no modest matron or maid had pulled the blind down. It had been Dr. Rendall's study blind, whipped down obviously by the doctor himself the instant he heard a strange footstep, and now raised again. Why had it been dropped? What had it hidden? In the look of the room itself there was not a suggestion of an answer to either question. It was just an ordinary man's study, a cross between a smoking room and a library, a much more comfortable room than the outside of that house promised. Yet people do not suddenly pull down blinds in the middle of the forenoon for no reason at all.

For a moment I thought of a passage at arms with a pretty housemaid as a solution. But it would obviously have been much quicker and simpler for any other party to flee the room than to make for the window and lower the blind. No; something had to be done which took a few minutes to do. I thought instantly of one possibility - the folding up or putting away of maps or plans. No doubt there were several other possibilities, but there seemed the best of reasons for not giving these worthy gentlemen my confidence. In fact quite a different course of action suggested itself.

Transfixing the doctor suddenly with a significant eye, I demanded in rather a low voice, "Are there many sheep in this island?" I still think it was a shot well worth risking, but to be quite candid it failed to come off. At least it did not come off entirely. Both the gentlemen certainly looked a little startled, but all Dr. Rendall did was to stare at me very hard, while O'Brien exclaimed.

"Faith, he's a dealer!"

But again I refused the proffered explanation, even though it was quite evidently the easiest way of accounting for myself.

"No," said I, "but I am very greatly interested in your beautiful island, Dr. Rendall. What a convenient spot to own!"

I still threw a touch of significance into my remark - especially on the word "convenient" - but this time I got a wholly unexpected answer.

"But I am sorry to say I don't own it," said the doctor. "I am afraid you must be mistaking me for my cousin, Philip Rendall. He's the laird; I'm only the doctor."

"The damned doctor," added Mr. O'Brien with a grin.

I began to apologise, but O'Brien who was by this time in capital spirits, interrupted me with,

"Faith, you needn't apologise, Mr. Merton. As long as you're not one of my damned relations I'm delighted to see you, and the doctor here is always pining for a fresh face. He's getting sick of mine!"

This remark seemed to have a spice of malice behind it, and the doctor certainly frowned, but I was so anxious to seize this opportunity of putting a question or two that I did not stop to wonder what was implied; not, at least, till afterwards.

"I suppose you have little society in this charming island?" I suggested.

O'Brien was certainly ready enough to give me exactly the information I was after.

"There are just four civilised houses in the whole place, counting this," said he. "There's the laird's - and saving the dear doctor's presence I must say his cousin is a damned queer fish, besides being as poor as he's cranky, and there are the two ministers, only one's away and the other's as dry as my own throat's getting. What do you say to a drink, doctor?"

He grinned at Dr. Rendall with a malicious significance I could make nothing of. I could see that it perturbed the doctor, who answered in evident embarrassment,

"If Mr. Merton would care for a glass of lemonade"

A hoot of laughter interrupted him. It reminded me of

Jock, except that Mr. O'Brien's laugh had such a flavour of ill-nature. The man might or might not be what I suspected, but he was indubitably objectionable.

"No, thank you," I answered him. "I set out to call on Mr. Rendall and the time is passing."

"Damned pleasantly in our society, eh?" put in O'Brien with the same sardonic laugh.

They both saw me to the door, and we said good-bye, without enthusiasm on the doctor's part, with a grin on Mr. O'Brien's, and with very mixed emotions on my own.

VI

A PETTICOAT

I was very thankful to get out of that depressing house and away from Mr. O'Brien's laugh, and yet hardly was I on the high road again before I was blaming myself for not having lingered longer and pursued my investigations there a little further.

The other "Civilised" households in the island apparently numbered only three. Now, if my spy were working single handed he might conceivably be some better educated farmer who had lived abroad and turned traitor, but it seemed to me most unlikely that he should have no confederates, and it was scarcely possible for two or three men of that particular type to be gathered in so small a community. Brains and education seemed implied in every step of the dangerous game they were playing. Therefore it was only common sense to suspect one at least of these "civilised" houses, unless they could all manifestly clear their characters. Anyhow it were foolishness to neglect this consideration.

And what had I discovered already? A couple of men living by themselves in a criminal looking mansion, who hurriedly pulled down blinds, looked both suspicious and apprehensive at the sight of a stranger, and made odd innuendoes and allusions in their conversation. Why hadn't I stayed on and pursued my investigations? Well, because the moment I discovered I was in the wrong house, my insistent idea was to push on to Mr. Rendall's and consult with him about the whole situation. But now I began to reconsider this decision very seriously.

I was out of sight by this time in a secluded part of the road, where it ran through a dip in the ground, with the head of one of those little reedy lochs only a yard or two away, and a bright glimpse of the sea beyond. The marshy shores were a perfect blaze of yellow wild flowers and it looked so jolly that I sat down on the water's edge and began to think things over.

First I thought Mr. O'Brien over. Middle height, a beard, and an Irish brogue. Could the German accent have been put on to conceal the brogue? Looking to what I was doing myself, why not? Then I thought Dr. Rendall over. Also middle height, a moustache, and no particular accent. But then again, if I put on an accent, why not he? Then I thought over what I had learned of the laird. A cousin of the doctor's, a "damned queer fish," almost the only associate of this couple, and hard up. Ought I to go straight off and confide in him?

"Not to begin with anyhow!" I said to myself, and up I jumped and continued my walk.

About a hundred yards further on I rounded a corner and came upon a very miserable figure. He was an old, old man with tinted spectacles and a long white beard, and the raggedest overcoat I ever saw, and he was sitting on the grass with his feet in the ditch apparently doing nothing but simply sitting still. As I approached he peered at me as though he were more than half blind and then in an extraordinary thin, high, piping voice he said,

"A fine day, mister!"

This time I did the Teutonic bully. It went horribly against the grain to strafe such a miserable object, but with no one looking on I thought that the kind of Hun I was supposed to be would probably treat a worm like this to a touch of the All-Highest.

"Be dashed and damned to you!" I growled.

The old boy started perceptibly, and in rather an eager voice he asked,

"Have you got a wax match, mister?"

"Wax match? No, and be confounded!" said I.

For the next quarter of a mile or so I felt too ashamed of myself and too contrite to think much about what the old fellow had said, and then suddenly it began to strike me that a *wax* match was rather a curious thing to ask for. A match was natural enough, but why need it be wax?

And then I stopped, wheeled round, and walked back. I told myself that I was growing absurd and getting passwords on the brain. Still, there seemed no harm in exchanging a few more remarks with the old man.

But when I reached the same spot on the road he was gone. There were one or two small houses not far away and it was quite possible he had reached them by now, especially if he wanted his match badly; though it would mean moving a little faster than I had given him credit for. Or he might be lying down out of sight having a nap, and as the day was warm and he had apparently nothing better to do, that seemed a very possible solution. Anyhow, there was no sign of him, and if there had been, I told myself he would probably have proved to be merely the island patriarch with a senile fancy for wax vestas, so I resumed my journey to the "big house."

As I topped another rise I got the best view I had yet seen of the lie of the island. A group of larger buildings on another hillock, still well over a mile ahead, was evidently the mansion at last. Behind me I saw the doctor's house and noted with a nod unto myself that it stood distinctly in the northwest district of the island. It was no long walk from that bleak habitation to the Scollays' on the shore.

And now I addressed myself to a delicate question. If I were going to keep up the part of suspicious stranger at the Rendall's, at all events to begin with, what account of my arrival should I give? It must be a tale plausible enough to keep them in doubt, for unless the laird himself were actually up to his neck in treason (and though I was prepared for anything by this time, there were limits to the assumptions I ventured to make), he would certainly wire either to the police or the naval authorities and I should immediately become a mere spectator. In fact, I would probably not be allowed even to stay and look on.

And this was not mere selfish desire for glory and excitement. I was quite capable of seeing that my tale might not convince older and wiser people as thoroughly as it convinced myself. In fact I felt a strong presentiment that I should merely be put down as a brilliant liar and the spy hunt would come to an end - *with the spy still in the island.* That was where I still do think I was justified in playing the hand myself.

But what tale could I tell? The truth - that I had dropped out of a balloon? Who would believe it for an instant unless I produced the hidden parachute? And if I unearthed the parachute the whole island would know in a couple of hours and the people I was after would also be convinced. And it would not be a conviction that I was a fellow Hun.

And then I chanced to turn my head and I had an inspiration. About five miles out to sea I saw a ship, quite distinctly enough to spot her as a cruiser of much the same type as the ship I had soared out of yesterday. I filled in the details of the inspiration as I walked and when at last I saw her head away into the far distance the final touch was given.

When I drew near the house the road showed a tendency to meander, and as I was getting pretty hungry and counted on luncheon with the laird, be he patriot or traitor, I left the highway and followed a path across a clover field. Though the house and its farm were so near, and I could see half a dozen other homesteads not far away, yet there was not a living soul in sight, or any sound save from the peewees and the gulls. I don't know how to convey the impression of out-of-the-worldness and back-of-beyondness produced by this sense of silence and space, and by the look of the house and its whole surroundings. The path sloped up to it through a grass paddock, rather like the approach to the doctor's house, only this grass was short and well-tended and there were one or two flower beds before the door and ivy on one of the walls (where the wind was least destructive); and though the mansion was weather-beaten and plain and grey, it had nothing of the bleak and chilly aspect of the other house. It simply looked as though it had lived a long and stormy life and had now gone to sleep.

At one side stretched a high-walled garden with the tops of a few stunted trees just showing their heads, and close at the back of the place one could see a collection of farm buildings, very like the mansion architecturally, only greyer and more weathered. A fairly steep roof, crow-stepped gables, rough-cast walls, and rather small windows seemed to my untutored eye to be the chief features of the whole stone gathering.

"Somebody very primitive obviously lives here," I said to myself as I pulled the bell.

Out it came bodily in my hand, so I carefully pushed it back, and tried a large brass knocker instead, a massive affair that looked as though it had once been part of a shipwreck. I knocked once, I knocked twice, I knocked thrice, and then the door opened and I enjoyed a fresh sensation.

Instead of the prehistoric being I had expected, a girl stood in the open door looking at me out of a quite remarkably bright pair of eyes - disconcertingly bright in fact. She was dressed in the very smartest and most-up-to-date country kit; short tweed skirt of a pleasing greenish hue, stockings to match, brown brogued shoes, and a blouse that might have come from Paris. Her hair was dressed as fashionably as the rest of her, and her face was of precisely the kind I had least expected to see, rather thin with neatly chiselled features and delicate eye-brows, and an entirely sophisticated expression. There was no doubt she was decidedly pretty, and quite delightfully fresh and trim looking. But her eyes were her best feature. As I looked straight into them for an instant I could scarcely bring myself to play the part I had arranged. They seemed as though they would be a little difficult to deceive.

However, thank Heaven I have lived down most of the virtues that embarrass the young. I had lied before, been found out, and lived through it; so I clicked my heels together, bowed, and enquired,

"Is Master Rindall in?"

(My accent wasn't really quite as bad as that, but I should have to invent fresh vowels to illustrate what it actually sounded like.)

I had expected some slight symptoms of alarm, but she answered with perfect composure and in a voice that matched the hair and blouse,

"Yes, he is. Will you come in?"

I bowed again and entered the mansion of Mr. Rendall.

VII

AT THE MANSION HOUSE

As I followed the girl through the hall, a man's voice asked,

"Is that O'Brien?"

"No," she said, "it's some one to see you, father."

She showed me into a room and closed the door, and in the course of the next few minutes I came to one or two pretty obvious conclusions. She was clearly Mr. Rendall's daughter, and they were equally clearly in the habit of receiving visits at odd times from Mr. O'Brien; in fact they evidently concluded it was he, or Miss Rendall herself would scarcely have opened the door to me. Also, her reply might be taken as implying that if Mr. O'Brien had been the visitor, it would not have been her father he had come to see. But whether or no this were the true interpretation, I so thoroughly disliked and suspected O'Brien that any suggestion of intimacy was alone enough to make me glad I had started on the defensive.

"Otherwise," said I to myself, "what a charming girl to find in such a place!"

However, I reminded myself that I had not come here to be charmed, and proceeded next to take stock of the room.

It was not large, but pleasantly proportioned, low in the ceiling, and pervaded with a delicate yet distinct flavour of the past, I found myself instinctively wondering how one could reproduce this particular flavour on the stage; no armour or tapestry or any of the usual antique paraphernalia to be allowed, for beyond the thick walls and rather small windows, it was so difficult to lay one's finger on any one specific thing that palpably suggested age. Finally I decided that it was impossible to re-create such an atmosphere. It was compounded of stillness within and the glimpses of primeval quiet without, of a touch of comfortable shabbiness, of plenty of elderly books, and of a faint odour of the dampness of centuries mingled with the scent of honeysuckle. My suspicions were suddenly lulled, and with that prompt decision which has landed me in and pulled me out of so many holes, I decided to drop my German accent. That the charming Miss Rendall might miss it, and wonder what had become of it, was (I must confess) a reflection which did not occur to me till afterwards.

Just as I had come to this decision, in walked the laird, and in two minutes I had come to another decision, which was to adhere to the plan of campaign I had thought of as I walked, in so far as keeping my business to myself was concerned. My first impression of Mr. Rendall was of height, and a certain quiet, formidable quality. He was grey-haired, with a close-clipped grizzled moustache, loose clothes as though he had shrunk a little in girth, and the unmistakable air of a man who had seen considerably more of the world than the island of Ransay. He received me quite politely and hospitably, but with every moment that passed I grew more acutely conscious of something deterrent behind his courtesy. A sense of a strong personality in the background, not actually hostile as yet, but ironic and critical, set me instinctively and instantly on guard. Not that I actually suspected the man; but to take him straightway into my confidence was simply impossible. A man of another temperament might have done so - and quite possibly have been right; but his effect on me was like tapping a limpet.

I gave him my name and then I said in a quiet confidential way,

"Forgive this intrusion, Mr. Rendall, but the fact is my ship has evidently been called away."

I glanced towards the window, and following my look he could see the smoke of the cruiser just visible on the horizon. He gave a little nod but said nothing.

"I was landed last night on a certain piece of business," I went on, "and it is no part of that business to make myself conspicuous, and so I have taken the liberty of coming to your house."

"You wish to wait here till your ship returns?" he enquired.

"I thought perhaps you might know of some lodging where I might remain quietly."

He smiled slightly.

"You had better stay here. There is no other lodging."

I began to thank him, but he cut me short.

"It is Hobson's choice," said he, "and my house is not overcrowded at present. Have you lunched?"

"I am afraid I haven't."

"Come and join us. My daughter and I had just sat down."

He moved towards the door.

"I have no luggage," I said.

"I can lend you what you want."

I thanked him again, and said brazenly,

"May I ask for the loan of a coat. I am anxious not to exhibit my uniform coat in the island if I can help it."

I thought he looked a trifle surprised (it must be remembered that all this time I was in a buttoned-up oilskin), but he merely nodded again and led me upstairs to a pleasant bed-room with a low ceiling and some heavy old-fashioned mahogany furniture. There he left me and in a moment returned with a brush and comb and a tweed coat.

I had noticed that in one of the drawers there was a key, and as I took the coat I said,

"I hope you won't think me unduly cautious if I lock my uniform coat up in one of these drawers. There are certain papers in the pockets which I am bound to be careful of."

Again I fancied I caught a brief look of surprise, but it must have been very brief, for his face was as inscrutable as ever as he answered,

"Do exactly as you like."

A maid came with a jug of hot water and then I was alone.

"I wonder if the man believes me?" I said to himself. "Things are going a little too dashed smoothly!"

However, there was nothing for it now but playing the game out. I first took the precaution of suddenly and quietly opening the door. There was nobody at the key hole, so I took off my oilskin and put on the tweed coat, and then locked up the top drawer and put the key in my pocket. Hardly necessary to say that drawer remained as empty as the others.

"I call that either a very neat dodge, or a devilish silly one," I said to myself. "And which it is depends entirely on the results."

As I brushed my hair I thanked my stars I was fair, for a shave was now long overdue.

"What a pirate I'd look if I were a brunette!" I thought, and as it was, the recollection of dainty Miss Rendall made me determined to borrow a razor forthwith.

I foresaw that lunch would be a function demanding considerable tact. Seeing that I had decided, rightly or wrongly (and the Lord knew which!), not to trust these people, they had to be kept in a nice equilibrium betwixt doubt and confidence. To persuade them too thoroughly that they were entertaining a genuine British naval officer would be fatal if they were treasonably inclined, and a serious mistake if they were not, for then they might reassure the other islanders and my gang would go to earth, not to be dug up again in a hurry. On the other hand, to have them too suspicious would be all right if they were treasonable, but would probably end my adventure if they were honest.

The line I selected was a blend of mystery regarding my business, breezy chat on non-committal topics, and an occasional oddity of conduct, such as might have been caused by a guilty conscience or a harmless strain of eccentricity (and I left them to make their choice).

Here are a few choice excerpts from our conversation, which I happen to remember more or less verbatim.

Myself (chattily): "Delightful air you have in your island! Like champagne - or perhaps in these parts I ought to say like whisky and soda."

Mr. Rendall (somewhat drily): "We do happen to be acquainted with champagne."

Miss Rendall (smiling pleasantly as she ate): "We probably don't look as though we were, father. Mr. Merton's metaphor was safer."

Myself (feeling rather an ass, but outwardly gay): "I meant no reflection on your cellar, Miss Rendall. I was merely aiming at local colour."

At this point I fell abruptly silent, the laugh, as it were, frozen on my lips. I gazed at my plate and then glanced furtively at my host (I was giving them their choice). The next fragment of conversation which I remember ran somewhat thus: -

Myself (leading up deliberately to the test question): "There's one thing I envy the natives of this happy island. What a wonderful show of wild flowers they have! Do they make good grazing?"

Mr. Rendall (again drily): "If one happens to have ruminant tastes, I believe they are edible."

Miss Rendall (brightly, but evidently unkindly): "Mr. Merton was probably thinking chiefly of the ruminant natives."

Myself (keeping sternly to the point): "I was thinking chiefly of sheep." *(With a direct and steady look at the laird.)* "Are there many sheep on this island?"

Mr. Rendall (quite calmly): "A good many. Are you anxious for statistics?"

Myself (concealing my disappointment under a brave smile): "Oh no. Please don't mistake me for an intelligent enquirer."

I turned the brave smile on to Miss Rendall. She smiled back very slightly. In her face I seemed to read a trace of scepticism; as if she did not quite agree with my modest estimate of myself, but at the same time thought none the better of me. I would have given a good deal to know exactly what was in her mind. Did she suspect something? And if so, what?

I had one more shot. It was an inspiration which came

to me at the end of lunch when my host offered me a cigar.

"Matches?" he observed, pushing a box towards me.

Again I looked at him hard and asked,

"Have you such a thing as a *wax* match?"

His eyebrows rose slightly.

"If you prefer to light a cigar with a wax match I daresay I can find one."

"If Mr. Merton doesn't mind waiting for half an hour perhaps I might discover a box in the store room," said Miss Rendall, and she added demurely, "beside the champagne."

My only consolation was that I was making an idiot of myself in a good cause.

VIII

SUNDAY

I said good-night early that evening and did a heap of thinking in my bed-room. Nothing that seems to me now to be worth recording had been said or done since luncheon. I went for a solitary walk in the afternoon, as much to carry out the part of one with some business in the isle as for any other reason. It is true I actually did do some business in the way of accosting a few inhabitants and trying tactfully to convey a suspicious impression. None of them, however, had seemed in the least likely to belong to the gang I was after, and the sheep and wax match conundrums had left them cold. I was the less concerned at this since I had realised that the day was Saturday. To-morrow in church I meant to take stock of the islanders - and give them a chance of taking stock of me.

That night my thoughts ran chiefly on my host and hostess. I had learnt a few more facts about them and these I now put together to see what picture they suggested. In the first place, the Rendalls were an ancient family in these parts and had owned their property for some centuries. As all my prejudices ran in favour of old families, old port, and old furniture, this was so far reassuring.

On the other hand, Mr. Rendall had apparently lived much abroad but he dropped no hint as to whether he had sojourned in foreign parts for reasons of pleasure, health, or business. In fact he was close as a clam on the subject, and, indeed, on every other subject. Add to this that I had heard he was hard up, that he had no wife to look after him, and that he evidently took a caustic rather than an enthusiastic view of life, and in my present state of mind there seemed a *prima facie* case for suspicion. Anyhow he was a man to be watched.

As to his daughter, I had learned that her name was Jean, that she had been to school at a somewhat select seminary which I chanced to have heard of, and that she had finished her education a couple of years ago in Switzerland.

"Nothing very suspicious in all that," I thought. "Still, what is this surprising apparition doing in this out of the way island? 'Looking after my father,' she'd say. But why look after him here instead of some more amusing place. Perhaps because they are hard up. On the other hand, perhaps not."

Then I thought over the pair simply as one thought of any new acquaintances before war was dreamt of, and I am bound to say they came out of the ordeal very creditably. He was well born, well bred, and very far from a fool. She was - well, I don't mind confessing that that night I considered her charming, in spite of the pretty obvious fact that she was not at all charmed with me. Or if she was, she concealed her feelings admirably. She had a good enough excuse, either way; whether she were honest and thought me a traitor, or whether she were treacherous and thought me honest.

Besides, I had not yet shaved.

So I forgave Miss Jean her prejudice and reflected on her attractions. I changed my mind about them later, as will appear, but that first evening she seemed to me a most piquant and dainty young lady. Slim, trim, and demure, with eyes like stars (I borrow the metaphor unblushingly), and a pleasant spice of mischief in her tongue, and a touch of the devil very carefully and properly hidden away; that was my first impression of Miss Jean Rendall.

And then I turned in, and slept that night without a dream.

Sunday was another gorgeous day. The breeze had almost quite died away, the sea glimmered through a heat haze, and the colours of the wild flowers were brighter than any palette. I came down shaved, but found Miss Rendall still cool, and her father as inaccessible as ever.

"Anyhow," I consoled myself by reflecting, "I have eliminated my bristles as a cause for my unpopularity. They have something else on their minds!"

The laird lent me a felt hat and as the hour of noon drew nigh we set off for the parish kirk. There was another church in the island (as in every self-respecting Scottish parish, I believe), but by the greatest good luck the rival minister was away and the congregations were assembled together. I gathered afterwards that this happy result was partly due to the hope of seeing the laird's mysterious guest, and that several very prickly theological scruples were swallowed by divers of the other congregation. At all events the church was crowded and I had the chance I wanted.

As we approached the kirk I thought I had never seen a plainer, more primitive little building even in a Scottish kirkyard; no spire, no ornament, nothing but grey roughcast walls (what they call in Scotland "harled") and a roof of small yellowish flagstones, set in a bed of mingled nettles and tombstones. Amid the tombstones stood the congregation, all in black and staring steadfastly at the mysterious stranger, while over the door a plaintive little bell creaked and clanged.

We entered the little church and I shall never forget my surprise. It was the year 1914 without; it became the year 1514 (or perhaps some centuries earlier still) within. On one side two minute windows pierced a wall quite four feet thick. The other wall was broken only by a great empty niche whence an image once adored had vanished. It is true there were now pews, but they were not of yesterday - square boxes where people sat and faced in four directions, and the odour of damp bibles smelt prehistoric.

The bell ceased clanging, the people trooped in and filled the boxes, and presently there uprose in the pulpit a grim venerable man in black. By this time my better feelings were under control and I studied this figure critically. He represented one of those four "civilised" and suspect houses. One was untenanted, two I had now visited, and the fourth I was now almost ready to discharge with a cleared character. Outwardly at least this sedate divine suggested nothing but the austerer virtues.

For two hours the minister prayed, the minister read

and the minister preached to us; at intervals we were allowed to sing, and abused the privilege shockingly; and all the time I studied that congregation. I recognised the Scollay family, Peter elder, Peter younger, Mrs. Scollay, the two rosy daughters, and even poor Jock. The three or four people I had spoken to in the afternoon were all there too. In fact I saw every one I had consciously met before in that island, with three exceptions. The doctor and O'Brien were not in church, and narrowly though I looked, I saw no sign of the ancient with tinted spectacles and a taste for wax matches.

I very soon was made aware that there was no fear of myself going unobserved. At one time or another I caught every eye in that congregation rivetted on me, and it only remained for me to give the proper impression to carry away with them.

As I was unable to see myself as others saw me, I cannot say precisely what effect I produced, but if a habit of looking suddenly and guiltily at the floor when I caught a hard staring eye, a conspicuous difficulty in following the order of the service and knowing what book to be picked up and whether to kneel, sit, or stand, and peculiarly unpleasant shake which I introduced into my top note - if all these manifestations failed to convey the impression that I was a very suspicious person indeed, well, all I can say is that they ought to have done so, and that that congregation must have been singularly deficient in the proper kind of imagination. Of course I could hardly expect a sympathetic signal to be actually made in church, but I did hope my performance would surely bear fruit before many hours had passed.

At last the service ended, the commons crowded out, and the laird and his daughter rose in their wake and greeted the minister on their way to the door. I noticed that they did not introduce me, and also that the Reverend Mr. Mackenzie regarded me - over Miss Rendall's shoulder - with a sternly suspicious glance. Evidently he had heard ill of me already, and hope burned higher. If the minister had heard dark rumours, surely the spies had! Or anyhow they would when that congregation had all reached their homes (if they were not among the congregation themselves).

We passed again through many eyes in the kirkyard, and then the Rev. Mr. Mackenzie and the laird walked together for a short way and I found myself alone with Miss Jean.

"I didn't see Dr. Rendall or Mr. O'Brien in church," I remarked.

"They very seldom come to church," said she.

"I gather that Mr. O'Brien is visiting the doctor," I observed.

"Yes," said she, in a tone that promised little further information.

"Has he been staying with him long?" I preserved.

"For some time."

"Old friends, I suppose."

She did not seem to hear me, and I gave it up - in the meanwhile; but to myself I said complacently,

"Some mystery here!"

Presently I remarked,

"There was another face I didn't see - the island patriarch."

She looked at me quickly.

"The patriarch - who do you mean?"

"An old gentleman with a white beard, tinted spectacles, and overcoat somewhat the worse for wear. He hailed me on the road yesterday and asked for a match. I imagine he must live somewhere near the doctor's house."

She looked very thoughtful for a moment and then said:

"There is no one in the island with tinted spectacles, and nobody in the least like that living anywhere near Dr. Rendall's."

I looked at her sharply.

"Are you quite sure?"

She seemed to think again for a moment and then said:

"Perfectly."

I had something to think about on my way home to lunch.

IX

AN ALLY

After lunch I set out by myself with pretty high hopes. It seemed to me inconceivable that men (or even one man for the sake of argument, though I felt sure there must be more), who were lurking here on the business this gang were engaged upon, would actually take no steps one way or the other to deal with a stranger who knew of their existence, and who to all seeming was one of their own kidney. I flattered myself by this time that every report they could have heard and every observation they might have made must incline them to the view that it was their duty to get in touch with me again. And now I proposed to take a solitary ramble along the very shore where I had stumbled upon my oil-skinned friend, and give them a chance of getting in touch.

It was an afternoon of sunshine and gleaming seas. At first the air was redolent of clover, and then - as I drew near the shore - of seaware. On this day of rest there was hardly any one to be seen about, so that a quiet meeting by the beach could be simply arranged. Only a meeting implies two, and though I walked right along the coast till I got within a stone's throw of the Scollays' farm I remained as solitary as when I started.

I turned back and slowly retraced my steps for a mile or so, my hopes fading and my perplexity increasing.

"What ought I to have done that I haven't done?" I asked myself. "And what have I done that I oughtn't to?"

I paused and sat down on the crisp sea turf with a rough stone wall to landward, and below me the shelving rocks and the glassy ocean, and it was then the idea struck me that I might do something to attract attention to my presence. A thoughtful aunt had presented me with a revolver when I got my commission, and as anything to do with hitting things, from cricket balls to pheasants, has always amused me, I used to carry it in my hip pocket regardless of chaff (one happily inspired wag dubbed me "jolly Roger"). I took it out now, descended to the beach, set up a stone as a mark, and proceeded to combine business with pleasure by doing a little fancy shooting. The thing made just enough noise to attract anybody fairly near at hand without scandalising the inhabitants, and as I chanced to be in good form I quite enjoyed myself.

I had just brought off a pretty sequence of snap shots and was thinking regretfully that in one of the happy lands which still encouraged the duel I should be a much more respected member of society, when I suddenly realised that I had a spectator of my prowess. He was standing on the turf above me, a little indistinct owing to the wall at his back, and for an instant my heart leapt and I thought I had met the friend I was seeking at last. And then I saw that it was only poor Jock.

I waved to him and he came scrambling down to the

beach, his mouth wide open as usual and wreathed in smiles. As he approached a wild thought struck me. He was bearded, thickset, and of medium height. Wrap him in an oilskin, and there you were! I mention all my inspirations to show that I really did cover the ground pretty thoroughly in that blessed island. It is true that the conduct of my oil-skinned acquaintance was scarcely that of a congenital idiot; still, I was resolved to leave no stone unturned.

"Shoots, shoots!" he babbled in his curious thick voice. "Jock heard shoots!"

I looked at him fixedly and in a serious voice replied in a German accent you could have cut with a knife,

"I vant to know zomezing about sheeps, Herr Jock, not about shoots. How many sheeps are zere in zis island, eh?"

Did I see a gleam of intelligence for an instant in Jock's eye? I cannot honestly say. I only know that he looked not unnaturally surprised, and then thickly answered what sounded like "A hundred and six." Anyhow it was nothing that seemed to illuminate the subject very brightly.

"And how many wax matches?" I enquired.

Jock hooted with laughter. He sounded so cheerful, that I perforce laughed too, and then I gazed at him sombrely.

"Jock," I said, "you are a fraud and a disappointment."

He laughed again , and then all at once a much more

sensible idea struck me. He was not a very promising ally, but he might prove better than none at all.

"Jock," said I, "I am a stranger."

He nodded and seemed to understand.

"Have you seen any other strangers in this island of yours?" I asked.

He seemed a little confused.

"No, no," he began, and then altered it into "Yes, yes."

Which did he mean, or did he mean anything at all.

" A man in an oilskin coat, with a moustache on his lip - here," I went on, touching my own lip. "Who goes out at night and walks along the shore; have you seen any one like that?"

Again he seemed to look intelligent, but he only shook his head vaguely.

"Well," I said, "if you do see any one like that let me know, and you will see some more shoots. Also I shall give you this."

I held up a new half crown and he laughed so joyfully that I began to have a faint hope he might prove of some use after all.

And yet when I had left him and resumed my walk back to the Rendalls' house, my spirits were not very high. As an ally Jock did not impress me with a feeling of great confidence, while his failure to recognise my description of the oil-skinned man depressed me unreasonably. I told myself that the opinion of the parish idiot on the subject of strangers was of small value. Besides, quite likely the oilskinned man would not be a stranger to the people in the neighbourhood. They might know him familiarly as a prosperous farmer or a hardy fisherman - or as their own doctor or their doctor's guest, or - no, he could not be their laird for Mr. Rendall was too tall. In short my talk with Jock had proved nothing one way or the other.

And yet my whole failure to come upon any trace of the gang in spite of all my ingenuity did set me thinking. Could it possibly be that my entire adventure had been an hallucination? I confessed frankly to myself that I have a pretty lively imagination, and I recalled vividly how I had almost collapsed on my way to the Scollays under the strain of an intense reaction, how my brain had whirled, and how I peopled the farm kitchen with full thrice the number of persons actually assembled. I had been conscious of all that, but supposing my brain had actually begun to whirl half an hour sooner, before I had become conscious of it? Might I not have imagined my whole mysterious adventure?

It was a nasty thought, for in that case what a superfluous fool I had made of myself since! But I faced it manfully, and sternly asked myself what the opinion of the average hard-headed, soberly reasoning man would be, if he were given the facts and requested to pronounce his verdict on them. What would be my own verdict if I were told such a yarn? Would I swallow it without demur?

"Be hanged if I would!" I said candidly.

By the time I got back to the big house, I had very nearly ceased to believe in the tale myself.

X

THE COAST PATROL

That evening we were all three sitting in the library (the same old-world room into which I had first been shown), when a servant entered and gave a message to Mr. Rendall. He rose and went out, leaving his daughter and myself each apparently immersed in a book. She may genuinely have been, but I was making the covers of mine a screen for inward debate. Had I made a mere fool of myself and should I make a clean breast of everything to my hosts? Or should I wait a little longer before deciding? I went on thinking after the laird had left the room, and Miss Jean still kept her eyes immovably on her page. I frankly confess I have never cut less ice with any woman - especially one who decidedly attracted me.

In a few minutes her father returned and said to her:

"John Howiseon has cried off to-night. I must go myself."

She started up with a word of expostulation, but he merely smiled in his grim way, nodded at her (not at me, I noticed) and was gone. With a little sigh she sat down again and plunged into her book, but my curiosity had been roused and in a moment I enquired,

"Is your father going out for long?"

Her concern seemed to have broken down her reticence

"All night," she said. "I wish he wouldn't!"

"What's the matter?" I asked.

"The coast patrol," said she.

"The coast patrol!" I exclaimed. "What's that?"

She seemed to look at me for an instant a little doubtfully before she answered,

"The Admiralty have asked all the Justices of Peace to have the coast patrolled."

"By whom?"

"Anybody they can get. We have the whole island mapped out into beats and the different; farmers take it night about."

For the moment I only half believed her. Such an amateur way of keeping watch and ward in such a vital area seemed hardly credible, but I learned afterwards that in those early days of the war that was one of the things which actually happened. Another fact also made me doubtful. On the night I landed I had met no watchers.

"Who watches the shore up at the north end - near the Scollays' farm?" I asked.

"Oh, Dr. Rendall and Mr. O'Brien look after that beat," said she.

In a flash my belief in my own adventure had begun to return. Either that couple neglected their duty - or I had met one of the watchers!

" Do the doctor and Mr. O'Brien ever go out themselves - like your father to-night?" I asked.

"Mr. O'Brien goes out pretty often, I believe."

I thought for a moment longer and then I jumped up.

"This seems the very job for an able-bodied young man," I said with a laugh. "I'm going out to join the watchers!"

"You!" she exclaimed, springing up too.

I looked her straight in the eye.

"Why not me?" I enquired.

She said nothing for an instant, and then she remarked in quite a matter of fact voice,

"Very well; if you are going, I'll come with you."

I could not resist parodying her.

"You!" I exclaimed.

But I got no smile in response.

" I'll be ready in five minutes , " she said as she left

the room.

"Now what the devil does this mean?" I said to myself.

Five minutes of course meant quarter of an hour, and then we sallied forth into the night, she in a long tweed coat and I in my inevitable oilskin.

"Which way do you want to go?" she asked.

"Suppose we work our way towards the north end," I suggested.

She said nothing more and we made our way by a track to the shore and then turned toward the left. I had been filling my pipe and when we got to the last stone wall, I stopped, bent under its shelter and struck a match. My face was towards her and in the fraction of a second before the first match blew out I caught a glimpse of something just visible in the mouth of one of the big pockets of her tweed coat. It was the butt end of a pistol.

I struck three more matches before I got my pipe alight and I contrived to face her each time, but she had turned and kept her other side towards me. When we resumed our walk I noticed that she consistently kept two or three yards away from me.

"Just shooting distance!" I said to myself.

"By the way, what are we supposed to be looking for?" I enquired presently.

"Chiefly periscopes, I think," said she.

I stopped short and gazed over the inky sea.

"Do they light them up for us?" I asked.

She laughed despite herself.

"That is what I've been wondering myself," said she.

This was her only sympathetic relapse, and to tell the truth I made no further remarks worthy of being smiled at. That pistol kept me thinking. That she had come out to watch me, and if necessary shoot me, seemed a pretty obvious deduction, and much as I admired her nerve, it made humorous conversation a trifle difficult.

On we walked, on and on for what seemed an interminable distance. It was quite moonless and only a few stars twinkled here and there through a veil of light clouds that had drifted up with the sunset. The grass underfoot was black, the sea was nearly as dark, and the inland country invisible. Once I remarked:

"It's a curious thing that we haven't met any of our fellow watchers."

"The beats are very long," she said, "and I'm afraid all the watchers don't keep at their posts all the time."

"What; they take a nap now and then?"

She seemed as though she were going to agree, and then to change her mind.

"Oh, we shall meet some one very soon. I think father is taking this beat."

But we met no one, and as we pursued our lonely way I began to think that here was quite a possible reason for my not having come upon one of these coast patrols two nights ago. Still, it was only a possible reason; the other alternative remained.

And then, I know not how it was, but I began gradually to get a curious impression that *something* was in the air, *something* was going to happen. It is easy to say I only imagine now in the retrospect that I had this feeling. But I noted the sensation clearly and positively at the time. I strained my eyes, I looked this way and that, so strong did the feeling become. Once I thought for a moment I heard soft footsteps somewhere on the inland side and I stopped short then and listened, but when I stopped I heard nothing.

It can only have been a few minutes after this that the figure at my side (which had been so silent that I had almost forgotten it was a girl, and a pretty girl too) stopped suddenly, and I stood still beside her.

"Do you hear anything?" she asked, and there seemed to be a little catch in her breath.

I listened and shook my head. I could see that she was gazing intently down at the beach.

"Do you see anything?" I asked in a voice instinctively hushed.

"No," she answered in the same low tone, "but I thought I heard something."

Again I strained my ears, and this time I distinctly did hear something; it might have been a movement among the rocks below, or on the bank ahead of us. She said nothing more but she seemed to be peering down into the gloom that veiled the beach.

"I'll go down and see what it is," I said.

For an instant I thought she was going to demur, but she said nothing, and with a bold air I stepped off the turf and began to make my way down, first through loose boulders and then along a ledge below. I confess frankly that I felt a trifle less bold than I looked, specially when I discovered the hazardous nature of the going. I remember that the sky began to seem lighter by contrast, but that the rocks were sheer chaotic darkness.

I must have been feeling my way along for some minutes, with a growing sense of the futility of the performance, when I first heard the sharp tinkle of a loose stone on rock. I turned towards the sound and heard it again. Either three or four times I had heard it distinctly when I found myself close to the grass again, only at this place there was a steep little cliff, higher than my head, between it and me, instead of a slope of boulders, so that any one on the bank above would be looking straight down on to me. All this I can swear to.

And then when my shoulder was rubbing this low cliff face, I thought - indeed I am sure - I heard something move above, and certainly there was a sharp grating sound on the rock at my back; within an inch of me, it seemed. I looked round quickly just in time to catch a glimpse of something thin and curved and sinister passing upwards, against the night sky. I did not see it descend again, but the next moment came the sharp grating, close to my head this time, and once more the long curved menace passed up, faintly visible against the sky.

I did not wait for it to descend again. That somebody was striking at me from above and that I had better get out of the way seemed so evident that I spent no further time in watching the operation. I started from the cliff, my foot struck a patch of seaweed, and with a half smothered "Damn!" I did the next few yards sliding seawards on my side. A peculiarly hard ledge stopped my career and for a moment I lay there wondering what bones were broken. By the time I had found there were none, and scrambled to my feet, the sky line above the bank was clear. Whoever had struck at me was gone and there was not even the slightest sound, save the gurgling of the sea below. And then I gingerly picked my way back.

I drew near the turf bank at the top and now again I stopped. Low voices reached my ear distinctly and presently I spied two vague forms standing close together. Before I moved again I had transferred something from my hip pocket to my oilskin jacket and I kept my hand there too, closed upon it and ready. Then I advanced.

"Is that you, Mr. Merton?" said a voice I knew.

"It is, Mr. Rendall," I answered drily.

"Did you see anybody?"

"No," I answered truthfully.

"We thought we heard a cry," said Miss Jean.

"I may have startled a sea gull," I suggested; and then I asked with a sharpness in my voice I could not quite control, "Where did Mr. Rendall spring from?"

"I told you I thought we should meet him," she answered, with a cool note in her voice that countered mine.

"What a curious chance that we should all meet here!" I exclaimed.

"It is precisely what I expected," said she.

"Did you think then it was Mr. Rendall down among the rocks?" I enquired.

"No," she said, "and it wasn't."

"Oh," I replied in a tone which (if I achieved my intention) might have meant anything - or nothing.

Her father had been standing perfectly silent during this bout, a towering figure muffled in a heavy ulster and scarf, with the rim of his hat turned down over his face. Now he spoke in his dry caustic way,

"Have you had enough exercise, Mr. Merton?"

"Quite, thank you."

"Then we can all go back together."

He turned and his daughter took his arm. I walked behind them - it seemed on the whole safer, and I kept my hand in my pocket all the while.

I had seen no one, it is true; I had heard no sound that could be sworn to as made by a human being, the thing I saw so dimly might possibly not have been a lethal weapon (and if it was a weapon, what in Heaven's name could it be? I wondered); it might conceivably have been a large bird some distance off, just as by a reverse illusion men are said to have fired at bumble bees when grouse driving. Also, it was within the bounds of possibility that the tinkling stones might not have been thrown down by some one above in order to draw me under that face. Everything had been so vague that all these alternatives were conceivable. But my own mind was quite and finally determined now that my adventure with the stranger on the shore had been no figment of my fancy, and I felt sure moreover that *they* had made up their minds about me and decided to act. How and why they had come to such a definite conclusion despite all my efforts to mislead them, beat me at first completely. And then I stopped short and almost shouted "Idiot!"

I had addressed Miss Rendall at her own door in a German accent. Then I had abruptly dropped it and through all my deliberate mystifications one fact had been clear - that I spoke in the accents of an ordinary more or less educated Englishman. The Rendalls clearly had the material for coming to a conclusion, and now in their company I had all but ended my days on earth.

Yet somehow or other now that I saw all this so clearly, I found myself singularly reluctant to accept the logical conclusion that this gentleman of good lineage and standing and this attractive high-spirited girl were actually traitors of the basest sort, and murderous traitors too.

"Hang it, I may be wrong after all!" I said to myself. "I know I'm young: I am told I'm rash; I have made a fool of myself periodically as long as I've known myself, I'll give them the benefit of the doubt a little longer."

At the door Mr. Rendall left us to resume his conscientious patrol. I said a brief and cool good-night to Jean, went up to my room and tumbled straight into bed.

"In the morning I'll think things over," I decided.

XI

A NEAR THING

Being an optimist has compensations. Indeed, it would need to have, for no virtue has ever landed any one in more damnable scrapes than optimism has landed me. But before the crash comes it does help to keep one happy.

Next morning, after that nasty night, I was singing in my bath and full of wild hopes; the fact being that a new and consoling way of looking at things had suggested itself in the very act of shaving.

"They are afraid of me!" I said to myself.

After a night's sleep the adventure by the shore had grown perhaps a little blurred in some of its details. I wished I could see that curved thing rising against the night sky a trifle more distinctly in my mind's eye; so that I could take my oath in court it was a weapon. Still, I remained perfectly assured I had been attacked, and the sustaining conclusions I now drew were, firstly, that "they" (whoever they were; and I tried to keep an open mind on that point) were so afraid of me that they were ready to stick at nothing to lay me out; secondly, that they were afraid to tackle me by day but had to choose a dark night and a lonely place; and thirdly, that with such a splendid chance it must have been nerves that made them bungle it.

"People in that state of mind will do something or other to give themselves away," I thought hopefully.

In this confident state of mind I came down for breakfast. My host, I found, was staying in bed after his night's vigil, and my hostess was daintier and more inaccessible than ever. After breakfast I reflected for a little over a pipe and then I asked her for a bit of lunch to put in my pocket and told her I was going for a long walk. She got the lunch and gave it to me without wasting a superfluous word, and off I set.

It was a breezy morning with a lot of thin cloud in the sky and a ruffled sea; cool and stimulating; the very day for a walk. I followed the exact route we took the night before, trying to identify such landmarks as rises and falls in the ground and sharp curves in the shore and farms close to the coast, but I found it was practically impossible; every feature seemed so utterly altered in daylight. My object was to find the spot where I had been attacked, and at last I had to be content with knowing that it must have been one of three or four places where the feature of a low cliff immediately under the turf was to be seen.

At one such place there was a long stretch of wall following the shore line, which could have given shelter for any one to stalk me practically from the start. At another I noticed a farm close by, and from this an assailant could easily have slipped down to the beach and run back again. At a third the configuration of the rocks was such that it would have been simple for him to have waited below the bank till he heard us coming, made a noise to bring me down, and then gone up above without exposing himself against the sky. In fact one could draw no definite conclusions at all.

Besides, there was the very distasteful alternative (and the more plausible it seemed, the more distasteful it grew) that there might well have been two people in it; one - who might have followed me, the stone thrower; and the other - who might, for instance, have been patrolling the shore from the opposite direction, the attacker.

Suspicious as I had felt at the moment, I shrank from this alternative, and in justification I asked myself,

"Why didn't she use her pistol, and be done with it?"

But, on the other hand, it was a most extraordinary coincidence that her father should have passed that spot certainly within three or four minutes previously, and that he should have seen no sign of my enemy. So far as I could remember the length of time I had spent groping among the rocks, it was just possible for Mr. Rendall to pass by and for the other man then to begin his work of decoying me, but certainly it was an unpleasant coincidence.

And finally there was a last alternative: that I might have been mistaken in thinking I was actually assailed and instead of that - But what other conceivable explanation could there be? I tried hard but could think of none.

With the flame of optimism burning now somewhat low, I kept on following the shore till I was well past the scenes of both my night adventures and had come to the little sandy bay with the huddle of low grey farm buildings just clear of the tide. I found Peter senior painting his boat on the shore and hailed him cheerfully with the same old guttural accent.

"Painting your boat, I see," said I.

He gave me a long look and one word.

"Ay," said he, and went on painting.

It struck me at once that he was even more wary and more reticent than before, but I was determined to extract some information.

"I have been guarding you against the Germans! Last night I patrolled your coast!" I informed him with great enthusiasm.

He looked at me rather curiously, I thought.

"Did ye see anything?" he enquired.

"I thought I did, but ach! how can one be sure in the dark?"

"It's no easy," he agreed.

"Then you have tried too, my friend?"

"Ay," he admitted, splashing on the paint.

"Were any of your family patrolling last night?"

"No," said he curtly.

"Who was guarding this part here?" I asked.

"I dinna ken."

I wondered, but I saw that there was not much more to be learned here. He had denied that any of his household were out, for what that was worth, and at that I bade him good morning and turned back.

I fell to walking more and more slowly and at last I stopped and decided to accompany my thoughts with a little lunch. The boundary wall at this point ran close to the edge of the rocks and was rather higher than usual. I thought for a moment of sitting down and lunching under its lee, and then I noticed that it was very loosely built of large beach boulders and that the off shore breeze was whistling through it like a sieve; so I decided to descend to the sheltered beach and lunch there. That decision saved my life.

I clambered down, chose a rock to sit behind, and was just putting my hand in my pocket for my packet of sandwiches, when "Crack!" - something whistled close to my head and smacked against a ledge behind me. "Crack!" again, and the smack this time resounded from the rock beside me. At the third "Crack!" I was flat on my face behind that rock and my hand was in another pocket. It brought out something more to the point than sandwiches.

I had a pretty good idea by this time where the shots were coming from and I risked a quick rise of my head to make quite sure. I just had time to see a flash through one of the holes in the wall and down went my head again as a bullet smacked once more upon the ledge behind. Yet another shot followed and seemed to miss everything, for I heard no sound of lead on stone, and then up went my head and hand together and I was covering that bit of wall with my own revolver. I saw that my enemy was no very dead shot and I meant to risk his fire and snap at the flash through the wall. I knew I could get quite near enough his peep hole to startle him, and after I had sprinkled the near neighbourhood of that aperture for five or six seconds I thought it probably odds against his keeping his head sufficiently to do much aiming. To be quite candid I must confess that it was a soothing sensation to feel I was the better man with a gun, and that I should have been in a proper fright if it had been the other way about. One hears a good deal of discussion on the quality of courage nowadays, and there is my own small contribution.

The seconds passed, my finger on the trigger and my eyes glued to the largest crevice I could spy in that wall, but there was never another flash or crack. And then it suddenly struck me that the man might be moving down the wall to get a shot at me from another angle. As usual I acted on impulse, and this time I think correctly. Scarcely had the thought struck me than I was up and rushing forward to the shelter of the grass bank where the rocks began. There, quite safe but rather cramped, I crept along parallel to the wall for about a hundred yards. And then I jumped up, charged the wall, and brought half of it down as I hurled myself over. As my feet touched the ground I looked in both directions, very nearly simultaneously, and saw - nothing.

Whether in that first instant I was more disappointed or relieved, I should be afraid to say, but as soon as I had had a few seconds to think, my one feeling was disgust that the fellow had given me the slip. I took to my heels and ran along that wall first in one direction and then in the other, but there was not a sign of a living creature. And the sickening thing was that by this time he might have done one of several things - headed away from the shore at top speed as soon as he ceased firing, in which case he would be far enough by now, or lain down in one of the several fields of corn near by, or crossed the wall further along and hidden among the rocks; and it was quite impossible to guess which. I pondered over the problem for a few moments and then decided that as it was perfectly hopeless to search the corn or the beach I would risk it and hasten inland on the off chance of getting a clue, so I chose a grass field and set off across it at a trot.

The ground rose for about fifty yards and then fell sharply, and as I topped this rise I came right on to a familiar figure. It was my friend Jock and he seemed unusually excited; almost, in fact, intelligent.

"Stranger!" he gabbled, pointing in the direction I was going. "Jock seen stranger!"

I followed his dirty finger and a couple of hundred yards or so ahead I spied a figure strolling along a by road, rather ostentatiously strolling, it seemed to me.

"Thank you, Jock," said I, "you're a good man! Here's your half crown!"

I dropped to a walk now and by the time the stranger and I met I think I looked about as cool as he did. It was Mr. O'Brien, as I had guessed at the first glance.

"Been for a walk?" he enquired.

"Having a stroll along the shore," said I.

He started a little and looked at me hard.

"Hullo!" said he, "I could have sworn you talked like a foreigner the last and first time I had the honour of meeting you. Were we both sober, do you think?"

I in turn looked at the man keenly. If his surprise was not genuine, it was as good a bit of acting as I ever saw, on or off the stage, and it was exactly the most disarming thing he could possibly say. Indeed it turned the tables on me completely and it was I who was now left in the position of having something awkward to explain away.

"It must have been the weather," I said lightly, "I'm never drunk before lunch;"

"And be damned if I get the chance at any time of day! You've heard of my sad complaint, eh?"

"No," said I, "I'm afraid I haven't. Nothing infectious?"

He gave one of his unpleasant hoots of laughter.

"Lord, you think I'm a respectable member of society then? Good for you, keep on thinking it - but you'll have to keep away from my friends!"

"It takes me all my time to keep clear of my own," said I.

His narrow eyes seemed to approve of me.

"You're not Irish?" he enquired.

"No; I've enough to answer for without that."

"You ought to be," said he. "You've got some wit. Damn the English, and double-damn the Scotch! Well we're evidently both going in the other direction, so good-bye to you!"

What was I to make of this? What was to be thought of the whole morning's adventure? Only one thing was perfectly clear to me: that I had a very dangerous, very determined, and very artful enemy in this island - or, almost certainly, several enemies, and that instead of the hunter I had become the hunted. They might fear me but they certainly did not fear to attack me whether by day or night. Had I sat down behind that trellis-like wall as I intended, I shivered a little to think of my fate. I should have been shot at twelve inches range, and that would have been the end of my spy hunt. I began to realise that it was much longer odds on my being dead within the next forty-eight hours than on my getting on the traces of that oilskinned man.

And then as I was walking back thinking these none too cheery thoughts, something put the parachute into my head. I had not thought of it before since the first night when I hid it. It took me a little time to get my bearings, but I found my way to the clover field at last and then made for the low wall with the bed of rank grass and docken leaves beneath it. I hunted up that wall and down that wall, but never a sign of the parachute was there.

"That is how they've bowled me out!" I said to myself. "They have heard by this time of the missing balloon; then they found the parachute, saw that the dates coincided, and spotted me!"

XII

THE KEY TURNED

When I got back I felt very little inclined for society. I passed through the hall as quietly as I could, went straight up to my room, and heaved a sigh of relief when the door was safely shut behind me. Perhaps my adventures had been following a little too quickly on the heels of one another; anyhow it was quiet which I craved at that moment. It was a reposeful room, scented with honeysuckle, and for a few minutes I enjoyed an unwonted sensation of peace; and then my eyes chanced to fall on the chest of drawers. I stared for a moment and then bent over the lock of the upper drawer, that drawer which concealed the mythical uniform coat with the important mythical papers in the pocket.

There could not be a shadow of doubt as to what had happened. The lock had been taken off and put in again since I last saw it. And now of course my hosts knew as well as I did that no uniform coat had ever lain there, and consequently that their guest had never worn one.

I had meant to slack, but this situation obviously required some thinking over, so I lit a pipe, threw myself down on the bed, and began.

J. Storer Clouston

"Bowled out again!" I thought. "At the rate the wickets are going down, the innings must be dashed near over. They've found out my German accent was a fake, they've discovered the parachute and know I neither landed from a British cruiser nor a German submarine, and now they know that I lied about that coat.

"And what is my own score? By Gad, I don't honestly think I've made a single run! I have no idea whether these discoveries have been made by people in league with one another, who pool their knowledge, or whether my enemies only know part of all this, and if so which part. However, that matters less since they know enough to shoot at sight.

"Furthermore, I don't know which of them are my enemies, or how many there are, or in fact any dashed thing about them. Therefore - "

At that point I fell fast asleep. My late night, the long morning in that stirring air, and the excitement of two missed-by-a-hair's-breath murders, had trundled me out again. The last wicket was down and the innings over as I slept. The one bit of luck I did have was not setting the bed on fire with my pipe.

It was about three o'clock when I went up to my room. It was 6-10 when I was awakened by a sharp click. I opened my eyes stupidly and looked all round the room. There was absolutely nothing to be seen there. Then with a strong presentiment I jumped up and tried to open the door. It was as I suspected. I was locked in.

My hand went to my hip pocket and found my revolver all right. They had not ventured to try and get at that. Then I began to wonder why the key had not been turned sooner.

"Something has just happened to make them lock the door," I thought, and thereupon I went to the window and looked out.

My room faced right down the island, the north shore to the right - the scene of all my adventures, the sheltered south shore to the left. Craning my head to the left I could just spy a small vessel of the trawler or drifter type lying close inshore. She seemed to be flying a white flag - it might have been the white ensign at the distance. And then I got a glimpse of three or four figures walking towards the house, and one of these wore a white cap.

"Now we shan't be long!" I said to myself. "But what the dickens does it all mean?"

About ten long minutes passed before I heard voices and footsteps on the stairs. The lock clicked again, the door opened, and there stood a square-shouldered man in dark blue, with three gold rings on his sleeve and a familiarly firm mouth and pair of steady eyes. For an instant I could scarcely believe my own eyes, and then I knew that it actually was - of all people - my own cousin. Commander John P. N. Whiteclett, R.N., whom I had last heard of two years before the war when he was on the East Indies Station. And behind him I caught a glimpse of Jean Rendall. There may have been others, but all I was conscious of was her eager face, the eyes brighter than ever, and the lips a little parted in tense excitement.

My cousin Jack spoke first.

"Good Lord, *you* of all people, Roger!"

"My dear Jack!" I cried, and then I checked myself and shut that door.

"Well," said my cousin, with more candour than politeness, "I always thought you would end in gaol, Roger, and you've had a dashed near squeak this time, let me tell you. What new form of lunacy have you bust out into?" His eye fell on my revolver. "And what are you doing with that thing? If it's going to be suicide, let me fetch in a witness before you begin. I hate being found alone with a body."

"Is that your ship?" I demanded.

"She's one of 'em. I'm boss of a few dozen of these floating palaces at present. In fact we're a patrol and I've caught you red-handed on my own beat, and what I want to know is what the devil are you doing on it? Not trying to elope with that little bit of fluff, I hope, because I can assure you she doesn't love you in the least, Roger."

"You mean well, old thing," I said, "but you've guessed wrong as usual, Jack. Take me to your ship, for the Lord's sake, and I'll tell you the whole yarn there."

"These good people probably expect a bit of explanation," he suggested.

"The Rendalls? Not yet! Wait till you've heard everything yourself. Tell 'em then if you like - but I don't think you will."

He looked at me curiously.

"Well," said he, "let's be off then. Don't you even want to say good-bye?"

"I'll send them a Christmas card," I said.

"What, after all the trouble they've taken to round you up?"

"Do you mean to say they sent for you?"

"Rather! Urgent wire."

The prospect of facing my grim host and his disdainful daughter struck me forcibly as less pleasing than ever.

"Come on!" I said. "I'm going to bolt!"

We went downstairs and out of the front door like a couple of burglars. The Commander did not appear to relish this performance particularly, but I went first and he had to keep pace with me.

At the door we found the escort provided for me, and very surprised they looked as they followed us to see their Commander so unaccountably intimate with his captive; but fortunately there was no sign of the laird or his daughter. I looked round me and felt sure I saw a well known slip of a figure standing against the weather beaten wall of the old mansion, gazing after us - with what sensations? I wondered very much.

"When did they wire for you?" I asked.

"Somewhere round about mid-day."

"And what did they say?"

"'They'?" repeated my cousin. "Why drag in the fair Miss Rendall? Her father did the wiring. At least I presume so."

"Assuming he did, what did he say?"

"Suspicious stranger come to Ransay - gave incorrect account of himself - that was the gist of it. Oh, he used the word 'urgent' I remember."

"Incorrect account? That was probably after they had picked the lock of my drawer and had something to go upon."

Again my cousin looked at me curiously.

"This sounds interesting," he said, and quickened his stride.

We reached a little unfrequented pier and jumped into the drifter's boat. Sitting in the stern I looked over my shoulder with very mixed feeling at the receding shores of the island of Ransay. It had baffled me, made a fool of me, nearly murdered me; but after all it had saved my life when the odds were a million to one against me, and it had crowded into that life the four most exciting days and nights I had ever spent.

XIII

ON THE DRIFTER

My cousin led me into the small deck house that served as his cabin when he was aboard. Through the windows we could see the afternoon gradually fading into evening, and the western sky turn crimson as we ploughed our way up winding sounds between the low-lying isles.

He produced a flask and a couple of bottles of soda water, lit his pipe, saw that door and windows were safely closed, and leaned over the table.

"Now," said he, "how the devil did you get to this place? That's the first question. They told me some yarn about a parachute, which I take it was really a hair net or a lobster pot - "

"It wasn't," I interrupted, "it was a parachute and I landed in it. Do you mean to say you hadn't heard of my disappearance in a runaway balloon?"

"What!" he exclaimed. "Are you the same Merton? I noticed the name of course, but do you mean to tell me they're giving away R.N. V.R. commissions as promiscuously as all that?"

"They give 'em to the pick of young England's manhood," I assured him. "The idea is to make the Navy into a real live force, capable of originality and enterprise."

He grinned.

"They've struck the originality all right," he admitted, "but, Lord, the time that will be wasted court-martialling you fellows! However, let's hear the whole yarn from the beginning."

I began at the snapping of the cable and told him my adventures faithfully down to the moment when he unlocked my bedroom door. He only interrupted once or twice to get some point or other clear, and then when I had finished he leaned back and looked at me hard across the table.

"Roger," he said, "I've known you long enough and well enough to know that you are not a deliberate liar, but I hope you'll forgive my saying that this is a damned tough bullet to chew."

"It sounds a tall order," I admitted, "but it's true."

He filled his pipe thoughtfully.

"I may as well tell you," he said in a moment, "that I am not at present a very credulous person. From the moment this blessed war began and I got this job, I have done little else than investigate spy legends, and I have come to the deliberate conclusion that there is either a lot more imagination in the world than any one has ever dreamt of, or that mankind are chronic and inveterate liars. I haven't yet had the luck to find one single true bill in any story I've investigated."

"Your luck has turned now, Jack."

"Possibly," he said slowly, "and mind you, Roger, there's no doubt whatever that a devilish secret service system exists; or that it's being used against us for all it's worth. Secret petrol bases for their submarines, secret signalling from the shore, mine-laying by so-called neutral ships; all that sort of thing is going on under our noses. I've got several very shrewd suspicions and hope to bring off one or two little discoveries not a thousand miles from this very spot. In fact, if you had pitched on any one of three or four other islands for the scene of your tale, or if what you'd seen had been just a little different I wouldn't have questioned a word of your story. But Ransay is not one of the suspected islands, and your friend in oilskins doesn't fit into anything I happen to have heard from other sources."

"Look here," I said, "what's the good of being cousins if we aren't candid? Do you or don't you believe me?"

John Whiteclett looked at me very steadily and spoke in his most deliberate accents.

"I believe that you believe every word of it. But I know you're an imaginative fellow and I can see for myself already that at least three quarters of your yarn can be explained away very easily."

"Explain it."

"Well, my dear fellow, just look at things for a moment from the point of view of a perfectly innocent and loyal inhabitant of Ransay - the Rendalls for instance. You appear on their shores absolutely mysteriously in the dead of night, you admit yourself you lay yourself out to behave like a thinly disguised Hun - d - d thinly too, apparently! You blow in from nowhere on the doctor and talk with a German accent. You blow in on the laird, begin talking with an accent and then drop it. You pitch him a cock and bull yarn about being landed from a cruiser and wanting to hide your uniform coat and so on. You conduct yourself like a criminal in church and wander out at night. Naturally the Rendalls - and everybody else - eye you strangely to your face and try to find out a little more behind your back. Do you see?"

"There's something certainly in all this," I had to admit.

"Then they find your parachute - "

"Who found it?"

"I haven't asked that yet; but I shall of course. Anyhow it was found, and as evidently you had hid it. One point discovered against you. Then the Rendalls decide on stronger measures - and very rightly too, I think. They open your drawer and find you never had a uniform coat at all. Most wisely they then wire to me, and to keep you from bolting, lock you in your room."

"Dash it," said I, "I seem at least to have succeeded in providing them with a devilish good excuse for every blessed thing they did!"

"I don't honestly think you have left yourself with any grounds whatever for suspecting the Rendalls of anything."

"On the other hand, sending for you and having me arrested would be an excellent way of getting rid of me when they were certain who I was - or rather, wasn't."

"And who did they make apparently certain you were not? A British officer! That was the natural conclusion when they opened that drawer. No, no, the Rendalls come out of it all right. Then let's take the doctor. He looks at you suspiciously - as well he might."

"Before I spoke!" I interjected.

"And do you flatter yourself that your appearance, without a cap and in a buttoned-up oilskin on a fine day, was reassuring?"

"But the blind?"

"Did you never see a blind come down with a run by mistake? There's a blind in my smoking room at home that comes down like that whenever you touch it. There's nothing against the doctor either - so far anyhow."

"And his friend O'Brien?"

"Ah, that's a different story. Mind you, you have shown me not a shred of evidence against the fellow. Still, what's he doing there? That's a thing I'm going to find out within the next four and twenty hours. But you can't prove that he *did* anything, and you can't suspect a man of treason just because you don't like his looks. There are possibly prejudiced people who don't like ours."

"Wait till you see him."

"I shall," said my cousin with an emphasis that hardly seemed to mean what I meant. "As for the Scollay family - nothing against them whatever, except that they live at a lonely spot on the shore, which I should say was rather their misfortune than their fault."

"And the old boy on the road, who, Miss Rendall declared, doesn't exist?"

"How long did you give her to run over all the inhabitants of the island? Did she look up a list of them, or a rent roll or anything?"

"No," I admitted. "Still, she seemed very positive, and she lives in the place and must know everybody. If she fibbed, that's certainly suspicious. If she was correct, then I met some one in disguise."

"Well," said he with an indulgent and extremely irritating smile, "I shall enquire about that old gentleman too. But, frankly, I've no doubt whatever that Miss Rendall simply forgot him when you asked her."

"All the characters seem cleared except mine," I remarked.

"Wait a bit, old chap. Now we'll come to the really suspicious things that you actually did see. First, the man on the shore."

"Can't he be explained away?"

"Possibly," said Jack imperturbably, "but he needs a good deal more explaining. You admit you became a bit light-headed soon afterwards."

"I've thought of that explanation myself, but it won't wash when he or one of his friends went for me on the shore."

"Are you dead certain anybody did try to go for you? You admit you saw nobody."

"I saw that curved thing - like a scimitar."

"But who on earth would be using a scimitar in these islands? And what a futile way to use it - jabbing down at you from overhead!"

"The point of it hit the rock hard enough."

"You had only the sound to go by."

"That's all," I admitted.

"And you heard that in the dark." He shook his head, "My dear fellow! I know you are telling me honestly what you *think* happened, but to be quite frank - "

He broke off and shook his head again.

"Well," said I, "that's explained away very happily. What I saw was only something else and what I heard was something else too. You put the alternatives so clearly, Jack, that one can't help being convinced. And what about the shooting affair? I only heard a thingumabob and saw a what-you-may-call-it, I suppose?"

"My dear Roger, I only want to test the alternatives and see what *can't* be explained away. Have you ever been under fire before?"

"No, but I've seen pictures of it in the illustrated papers."

"Dash it, be serious!" said he. "You have no doubt whatever that somebody blazed either at you or at something else from behind that wall?"

"Or at something else? What do you mean?"

"There weren't any duck about, or anything of that kind? I've known a wild shot blaze both barrels within six inches of my own head and explain he had never noticed me."

"I was rather too preoccupied to notice whether there were any duck there when he began," said I, "but unless they were deaf duck there certainly wouldn't be any left after he'd loosed off his first bullet. Besides one doesn't usually shoot duck with bullets."

"One might with a rook rifle."

"I admit that one might; also that a very excitable person might go on shooting after the duck had gone. But do you really mean to tell me, Jack, that that explanation satisfies you?"

"I don't say that it does absolutely, and I quite admit that the weakness of my explanations is that your story requires three of them; none being perfectly satisfactory. However, it comes to this, that we have narrowed the field down to three incidents that want a bit of explanation. Everything else points as much one way as the other."

"Which way?"

"To your being mistaken for a spy yourself."

A horried thought struck me. It was so horrid that it took a little pluck to get it out.

"In that case, supposing some patriotic individual had tried first to stab and then to shoot me, for his country's sake?"

"By Jove!" exclaimed my cousin and gazed thoughtfully into space for a bit. Then he said, "That's possible, but it's a tall order too; and it leaves out the man on the shore."

I was visited by another horrid thought.

"He might have been spy hunting!"

"Well, in that case we can easily get on to his tracks. There will be no point in his denying it. But would the conversation fit that theory?"

I thought for a moment and then said with heart-felt relief,

"No, it couldn't possibly."

My cousin fell silent and stared into the thickening dusk. Then he looked round with a start and said,

"We're nearly in."

We both went out on deck and saw at the head of the bay before us houses and lights on shore and a church tower against the evening sky.

"Well, Roger," said he, "I'll go into this business very carefully and make the most thorough enquiry. Don't think I'm not keen on getting at the bottom of it. You've got to get off at once and rejoin your ship of course?"

I said I must.

"I tell you what I'll do," he went on; "of course we've got to lie very low about this sort of thing, but I feel I owe you some account of what happens. I'll write and let you know as soon as I have finished my investigation."

John Whiteclett was the best of fellows, shrewd and level-headed and a first class officer, but somehow or other I felt small confidence in his getting the better of the cunning foe on Ransay. However, it was all that could be done now. My own part was finished and I had to confess I had failed ignominiously.

XIV

MY COUSIN'S LETTER

Three weeks later I received this letter from my cousin:

"My dear Roger,

"As I promised I am sending you a chit to tell you the result of our enquiry into the Ransay mystery. Of course you will understand that this is strictly for your own eye and mustn't be talked about.

"Well, I wanted to leave no stone unturned to get at the bottom of the affair so we got up a pukka detective from London, a man named Bolton, said to be a first class fellow at the job. He spent a solid week in the island and seems to have poked his nose into pretty nearly every house and spoken to pretty nearly every inhabitant from the laird down. Taking a tip from your tale he posed as a cattle dealer (which is precisely what he looks like) and of course he never let on that he knew of your existence - or mine either.

"The result of his enquiries is, firstly - nothing proved against anybody and no evidence of anything fishy going on in the place. This last point confirms my own experience, for, as I told you, I haven't yet been able to associate   this   particular   island   with   any   of   the suspicious ongoings which undoubtedly are happening.

"Secondly, your friend O'Brien turns out to be a gentleman with a failing for liquor who was sent up by his relations in Ireland about six months ago to live under Dr. Rendall's charge, there being no pubs in Ransay - and many in the island he came from. I find that it is by no means unusual to send thirsty souls to publess isles, and beyond the fact that O'Brien came up very 'convanient' for this war and is pretty free with his tongue on the subject of England's sins and shortcomings, there is really nothing positive against the man. However we are running no risks, and as we are God and Destiny rolled into one in these islands, we gave Mr. O'Brien his marching orders and by this time he has presumably either secured a drink at last or his friends have shut him up in some teetotal paradise a little further from the scene of war.

"Bolton's opinion is that O'Brien was without doubt the man who fired at you, looking to the type of gentleman he is, and the fact that you ran into him immediately afterwards, and especially the fact that he actually does possess an old rook rifle. He thinks he may have done it out of sheer Irish deviltry, you offering so convenient a target, just as they pot landlords in his own happy country. A man can hardly have drunk as heavily as he must have done without upsetting his brain a bit, and this theory seems to me not at all unlikely.

"Bolton thinks it hardly conceivable that O'B. can have had any deliberate idea of getting rid of you, since it is certain that he wasn't the man in oilskins you met the night you landed - or rather, dropped. He can't have been *because he doesn't know a word of German.* We ought to have thought of that clue ourselves. Bolton was on to it at once and points out that it puts out of court the whole inhabitants of the island except Miss Rendall who has a pretty good school-girl's knowledge of German, and her father who has been abroad a lot and knows a bit of the language. And apart from all other considerations, the man in oilskins can't have been either of them owing to their height. Miss R. is too short and Mr. R. too tall.

"Assuming therefore that you weren't a bit light-headed or anything of that kind (which, I am bound to say, Bolton thinks quite a likely explanation), the man you met *must* have landed from a submarine and gone away again in her. Bolton feels positive on this point, and I must say I agree with him.

"The only remaining difficulty is the attack on the shore. Here Bolton takes exactly the same line as I did when I questioned you. He thinks that as you didn't actually see anybody, and as what you think you saw and heard are so vague and indefinite and so difficult to fit into any known method of murder, one can't really draw any conclusions, and he quotes various cases he has known of people who fancied they were struck or seized or fired at in the dark, when actually there was some other explanation.

"By the way, as to the old gentleman with tinted spectacles who asked for a match, Bolton made enquiries of a number of people about the old men in the island, and he even took the trouble to interview them all. None have tinted spectacles and all deny having spoken with you. I am afraid that this discovery made him a bit sceptical about some of the other incidents. However he went into the whole thing very carefully indeed and I think we can all feel satisfied that with the departure of Mr. O'Brien the possibility of trouble within the island has been eliminated. Of course the Lord only knows who may not land in the place by night, and they may quite possibly have squared one or two of the natives to show a light, or to keep their eyes shut, or help them in one way or another. But that's rather a different story.

"I am sorry I have nothing better to satisfy your dramatic soul, but hang it, a fellow who flies from the middle of the North Sea in a balloon and then drops through a fog and hits an island a few miles square, and afterwards gets mistaken for a spy, and shot at and finally arrested, oughtn't to complain!

"Good luck to you. Keep out of balloons and don't part with that revolver.

"Yours ever,

"J.P.N. WHITECLETT."

And there for the present - and perhaps for ever - the story ends. I sat down straight off and began to write out this full, true, and particular account of the whole adventure, partly to keep my memory of everything fresh, and partly because it strikes me as not half a bad yarn in itself. Now that I have finished the job I must say that whether or no it will convince anybody else, it makes me feel more certain than ever that more has been going on in that island than met Mr. Bolton's eye.

Professional detectives are no doubt very useful men at jobs they are accustomed to and when pitted against the ordinary criminal. But these war problems are quite new, and utterly different even from the German secret service machinations in time of peace. And the men they are opposed to are very extraordinary criminals indeed; they are a highly trained, scientific force, as much a wing of the German fighting forces as their air service or their submarines.

What chance has a man who looks like a cattle-dealer against these experts, especially when he is only in action for a week and starts with the assumption that the few invaluable facts given him are mostly works of imagination? Possibly he may have fluked upon the remedy by removing O'Brien, and if the island of Ransay gives no more trouble for the rest of this war, it will certainly look as though he had. But in that case he will have been uncommon lucky, because he seems to me to have overlooked or dismissed practically everything significant.

Take, for instance, the actual words used by my oilskinned friend. They most distinctly implied that he was living on shore. Take the incident of the blind, which may perhaps have been, as John Whiteclett says, an every-day accident, but which certainly happened in the house where the one man they do suspect was living, and would certainly involve the doctor if it were not a mere accident. Look at my security while I was humbugging them by my suspicious conduct, and then the unscrupulous and quickly repeated attempts to get rid of me after two things had happened - my dropping of my accent at the Rendalls and the discovery of the parachute. Take that night on the shore when Miss Rendall escorted me armed with a pistol and her father joined her at the very place and the very time when the attack was made on me. As to its being an imaginary attack, my last doubts dissipated when I was fired at next day.

Then as to the idea of Mr. O'Brien trying to shoot duck, or suddenly being inspired by high-spirited homicidal mania, I simply decline to accept such absurd interpretations. I am not in the least sure it was he, to begin with. I feel convinced that more than one man is in it, and which conspirator took which part, who can say on the little evidence one has?

Again, take Mr. Bolton's brilliant idea of enquiring who could speak German. How did he enquire? Probably asked them! Is he a German scholar himself? The odds are a thousand to one against it. Or take the mysterious old man with the tinted spectacles. His appearance by that roadside and subsequent disappearance into space is one of the oddest features of the case. I have no doubt at all now that the wax match enquiry was the beginning of a series of questions and answers which would have proved me a fellow conspirator if I had only known them. They probably became doubly suspicious of me from that moment and only waited to make quite sure before going all out to kill me. And yet, Bolton by coolly assuming I was a liar or a dreamer missed the entire significance of the incident.

But when it comes to asking myself honestly which people precisely I suspect, and how I propose to separate the incidents which (I freely admit) are perfectly consistent with the theory that I was genuinely suspected myself, from the incidents which cannot be explained on those grounds, and work out a water-tight case against anybody in particular, I must confess that I am fairly beaten. I know that I don't want to suspect that girl, though she did treat me like a member of a lower race and scored off me badly at the end; and I do want to suspect O'Brien. By the way, was he a real drunkard? I rather begin to wonder.

And that is the very unsatisfactory end of the matter so far.

PART II

I

AN IDEA

I wish I had said that I felt sure my cousin's letter was not the last of the business on Ransay. One would like to be the only correct prophet this war has produced. It was not the end by any manner of means, as I learned within two days of finishing that last chapter. I wrote it, and the two or three before it, in the convalescent hospital at Winterdean Hall, finishing it, I remember, on a Wednesday; and I picked up the scent again on the very Friday following.

I had been laid out in an insignificant North Sea scrap, but though the scrap was small the wounds were unpleasant and I was still rather glad to lie easy in a moveable summerhouse on the terrace. I was well on the mend but had walked a little too far that morning and there I lay stretched half asleep in a deck chair, out of the wind and basking in the sun. It was the end of the first week in February, but the day was mild as milk and in my overcoat I felt positively hot. Rooks were cawing over the winter woodlands below the terrace, a faint, restful line of blue hills rose far away beyond, and a gorgeous peacock was strolling sedately on the lawn. I was utterly content to lie there and doze, when I heard a familiar voice.

"Right! I see where he is, thank you," it said.

"Jack Whiteclett!" I said to myself.

It was always pleasant to see Jack, but at that moment a bore to be disturbed. Little did I guess how thorough and final that disturbance was going to be.

He appeared in the open door of my shelter, keen eyes, blue serge, three rings, and all complete. I expected a jibe at my beard, but evidently I struck him too sorry and object for mirth.

"Well, old chap," said he, "you've earned a rest and I'm glad to see you're taking it."

This from Jack was subtily flattering and I did my best to look the wounded hero.

"Where did they get you?" he asked.

"In my beard," said I, "left side of the jaw. Also right ankle and a souvenir under the ribs."

"Lame?"

"Still a little, but improving."

"The beard is quite becoming," he observed.

"Look at it well then while you have the chance for they say they'll let me shave it in a week."

"You're well on the mend then?"

"Thank the Lord."

"Then I needn't give you any more sympathy. Congratulations instead."

"On getting a bit of Blighty?"

"On getting a bit of ribbon."

I opened my eyes, for this was the first I had heard of it.

"It isn't out yet," said he, "but I believe it's to be your doom. Somebody has presumably bribed some one at the Admiralty. Uncle Francis tipped me the wink. You've evidently quite made your peace there, Roger, so congratulations again."

This hint of a decoration was gratifying enough, and to hear, on top of it, his assurance that my dear old uncle had really opened his heart again nearly upset me disgracefully. I was evidently still a little weaker than I realised. However, Jack was tact itself and the talk turned to every-day matters.

He had been sitting beside me for some little time discussing the war, the world, and the devil, before it began to strike me as quite remarkably kind, even for so good a fellow as Jack Whiteclett, to come so far out of his way to look me up. His own wife was at Portsmouth last I heard of her, all his other interests were in London, and yet here he was looking up a cousin in a hospital a couple of hundred miles away from either place.

"By the way, how long have you got?" I asked.

"A week."

I sat up in my deck chair.

"Only a week! I say this is extraordinarily good of you to come down here and see me."

"Oh, I wanted to see how heroes bear their wounds," he smiled, but I felt certain there was something more left unsaid.

"Jack, old chap, what's up? I see in your eye there's something else."

He hesitated a moment and then said,

"There was, but I'm not going to bother you with it now. I didn't know how fit you might be."

Naturally I made him go on.

"Would it worry you if I were to yarn a little about that adventure of yours in Ransay?" he asked.

"Worry me! I've been thinking of little else since I came to this restful place. In fact I've been finishing off a full, true, and particular account of the adventure. Any further news?"

His mouth grew compressed and a frown settled over his eyes.

"Nothing definite, except that the infernal island has been worrying me a lot lately. You were quite right, Roger, and I withdraw my last doubt with many apologies. Something is very far wrong in that place. Submarines have been seen for certain two or three times, and signals on shore, and the devil knows all what. But we can't find a clue or a trace of anything to lay our hands on!"

"And all this is since O'Brien left?"

He nodded.

"Yes. If he were in it you were quite right in suspecting a gang. If he wasn't, then the fellow, or fellows, are still there. I am quite certain now, Roger, that you were absolutely right. Some one is actually living in that comparatively small island, and working a lot of mischief, and we haven't even the foggiest notion who to suspect."

"Have you applied to Mr. Bolton?" I asked a little maliciously.

"Damn Mr. Bolton! The fellow botched the whole business. He lost the scent while it was still warm, and now it's as cold as mutton and one has to begin all over again! I wanted badly to have a yarn with you about it, Roger. You may have some ideas. Bolton had none and I have none."

"Are you allowed to tell me exactly what has been seen?"

"I am not allowed, but I can tell you, if you won't repeat anything."

And so I may not go into particulars in this narrative. However, that makes no difference, for beyond indicating that the northwest end, out by the Scollays' farm, and the barren uninhabited tip of the island beyond, was the danger zone, these particulars gave no clue and suggested no fresh idea. Of course they naturally suggested people living in that vicinity, and yet this was far from inevitable because that coast was the best for the enemy's purpose, and his friend or friends on shore might come some considerable distance to get in touch with him. In fact, it would be a pretty obvious precaution to live as far from the scene of actual operations as possible; though equally obviously it would be a less convenient arrangement.

As for the precautions which Whiteclett was able to take, all that I am permitted to say about them is that, instead of the amateur coast patrol arrangement in vogue when I was there, a few men from a certain unit were put on to the job instead. But my cousin had no control over this, and as he alone realised - in fact, could realise - the peculiar danger on this particular island. The number of men spared for Ransay was very small (you could count them on one hand with something over) and they were but ordinary honest members of this unit at that - not experts at the game. Consequently he was a little doubtful whether the safeguard was any better than before.

Well, we talked the whole thing over and over again, and I honestly could suggest nothing to add to what I had told him before. And then I asked him,

"Have you yourself seen no cause whatever to suspect any one? Nothing happened - even a very little thing?"

He began to shake his head, and then said,

"Well, there was just one thing that made me suspicious for a moment, but then I came to the conclusion that my suspicious wouldn't hold water. A short time ago Dr. Rendall came in to see me and begged for leave to keep another drunk - what he called an alcoholic patient. He said he had heard of a man whose friends wanted to send him up to him, and offered to give me all sorts of guarantees of his honesty, et cetera, et cetera. I gathered that the doctor must be pretty hard up and this patient would make all the difference to him. In fact he practically told me so."

"Of course you said no?"

"I was sympathetic but told him I was afraid it was no good. I didn't want to seem too sharp with him, just in case he might be a wrong 'un and would be the better of a little show of guilelessness. Of course I let him know later he couldn't have the fellow. But honestly, Roger, I can't think there was really anything suspicious in his request. In the first place the trouble is going on without his inebriate. In the second place, the request would be too bareface if he meant mischief."

"Still," I said, "it shows the man is hard up. Suppose he has been tempted?"

"In that case we must also suppose he has fallen and pocketed a bribe; and then he wouldn't be hard up any more."

"One doesn't know his difficulties. He might require a lot to cover them, and be in need of a fresh cheque now. And there's one thing, Jack, that has made me wonder sometimes. He is a cut above the ordinary local doctor in such a place. What's he doing there?"

" Well, " said my cousin after a moment's thought, "the

problem in my mind always comes back to this, that we are never likely to get much forrader until we can station a spy of our own in the place to watch what's going on. And how can one possibly manage that without giving away who the watcher is? If they know who he is, he will find out nothing, and probably have his throat cut. That's the difficulty."

I said nothing for a moment. A brilliant idea was beginning to dawn upon my mind.

"Nothing to suggest?" he asked.

"I suppose," I said, thinking hard, "that if you had wanted to, you could have let Dr. Rendall have that man?"

My cousin stared at me.

"I shouldn't take the responsibility myself, but I daresay if I were lunatic enough to back him up, the powers that be might agree."

"Jack!" I exclaimed, "I'll be the alcoholic patient!"

For a moment I thought my cousin's eyes were going to start out of his head. Then they subsided and a grin began to steal over his face instead.

"By Gad!" he murmured.

"I'm the very man for the job! I've actually spoken to at least one of the gang in that island, apart from the old chap with spectacles. I know the ropes, so far as they are knowable. In fact I've a kind of prescriptive right to the job."

He nodded.

"I quite admit that you have; also that I'd sooner have you there than anyone else. Looking back, I think you had a most sporting try last time, and I must say it seems to me that only some devilish bit of bad luck prevented you from bringing it off. Though what actually the bit of bad luck was has often puzzled me. But then," he added, "you aren't the fellow he wants."

"One drunk is as good as another so long as he pays the fee."

"But supposing, for the sake of argument, he had some reason for wanting this other man. Would he take you in that case?"

"He must or he'd give himself away!"

"True for you, Roger. But how are we going to open negotiations without arousing suspicion? One might as well face all the difficulties."

"Oh, we can easily fix that up," said I. "My guardians will write and say they have heard of his excellent system, et cetera, and have hopes of making arrangements with the naval authorities, and so on. There will be no difficulty at all so far as that part goes."

"But, my dear chap, when you'd got there they'd spot you."

"With this beard - dyed black?" I cried, as inspiration trod on inspiration's heels. "And a pair of gold-rimmed glasses, and this limp - which will hide even my walk, and a complete change of clothes; who will spot me? Remember I was only there for a very few days six months ago."

"Your voice?"

"I only spoke in my natural voice to the two Rendalls; never to the doctor; in fact I've only met him once."

"But his cousins saw a good deal of you."

"I haven't been on the stage for nothing," I assured him. "I'll change my voice very little, not enough to make it difficult to keep up - throw in a lisp or something of that kind. You can trust me to do the thing thoroughly, Jack."

My cousin looked at me carefully.

"Yes," he admitted, "I think you are changed enough already to puzzle 'em; and with your beard dyed black - by the way, don't forget to dye your hair too, old chap! - and glasses, et cetera, by jingo I do believe you'll pass!"

"Now the thing is how to get permission: first, leave for me, and second, leave to land an alcoholic on the island. What about Uncle Francis - could he pull any strings for us? And will he if he can?"

"The very man!" said Jack, "if he really will take the thing up. He's in it with the best kind of big-wig for our purpose. And I rather think the idea might appeal to his sense of humour. Anyhow, I'll see him to-night when I get back to town, and failing him I'll try some one else."

And that was the abrupt end of those restful days, dozing in a deck chair listening to the cawing rooks at Winterdean Hall Convalescent Hospital.

II

A LITTLE DINNER

On the Tuesday evening, just four days later, I hobbled up the steps of my Uncle's club and put the same question I had so often put before to the same sleek benignant hall porter.

"Sir Francis Merton?"

He was as benignant as ever, but he handed me over to an attractive war worker with a detached air that showed he was quite unconscious of ever having seen me before. For an instant I was chilled, and then I realised the happiness of the omen. If my beard alone so changed me, there would be no fear of recognition when art had reinforced nature.

The only other guest had already arrived: - Commander John Whiteclett. My uncle was talking to him confidentially before the fire, and at the sight of that familiar upstanding figure with the dominating nose above the determined mouth and the fresh complexion and snow-white hair and genial eyes, all just the same as ever, I felt a sudden sense of confidence in the issue of my adventure. With such an ally at my back, the chances of failure seemed almost negligible.

"Well, Roger," he cried in his bluff strong voice (though I noticed it was discreetly lowered while there was any one within earshot), "I hear you've taken to liquor so badly that your friends have got to remove you from society! We always did think it would come to something of this kind; eh, Jack?"

"He always was a bad egg, sir," said my cousin. "I don't mind betting he hasn't brushed his beard."

"And that limp!" added Sir Francis. "Gad, I believe he's been kicked downstairs by an indignant husband!"

However, he pressed my arm as he laughed, and it was not a critical pressure.

"I can't shave owing to my shaky hand," I explained, "and the limp is port in the big toe."

"Port?" exclaimed my uncle. "No, no, my dear fellow, it's whisky poisoning you suffer from. You began in secret in your sixteenth year and have been a trouble to your friends since you were twenty-one. However, I've got all the particulars written out for you, and mind you get 'em into your head and don't contradict yourself or me when you go to live with that doctor fellow."

Jack winked at me from the shelter of our respected uncle's back and I hid a responsive smile. With all his virtues, Sir Francis Merton had never been fond of playing second fiddle, and this masterful seizure of our scheme and dictation of all the details was exceedingly characteristic. At the same time he was as shrewd as he was peremptory and I felt satisfied his details would be sound.

"It's all right so long as he doesn't insist on disguising himself too and coming with me," I whispered to Jack as we went into dinner.

"What I'm afraid of is that he'll go *instead* of you!" said Jack. "I never saw him keener about an idea."

We dined at a corner table whence we could see at once if any one approached too near, and I think my uncle must have arranged that neither of the nearest tables should he occupied; so he was able to get to work with the soup.

"I've arranged everything, Roger," he said, "you are on furlough so long as this job lasts. No questions will be asked and you'll have a free hand. Only of course Jack will always keep an eye on you, and I shall be able to advise both of you according to circumstances."

Jack winked again hurriedly, and said with as much deference as though he were speaking to an Admiral,

"That's very good of you, sir. I shall keep you in touch with the situation, for I take it it will be safer for Roger not to write more letters than necessary."

I glanced my thanks at him, and our Uncle, after frowning for a moment dubiously, agreed that he feared he must be content with hearing from the Commander only.

"But there will be no harm in my writing to you, Roger, now and then," he added.

"No harm at all," I agreed.

"Well then," continued our host, "we come to the specific arrangements. Only two persons at the Admiralty know of this scheme, but they are quite powerful enough to get you into this island of yours all right. Of course people who happen to hear of it may open their eyes a bit and talk of the slackness of our Naval Authorities, and it will do no harm, Jack, if you damn them a bit yourself - confidentially, you know, in case any one asks you how the devil this drunken fellow here has got into the place."

"If I simply give 'em my candid opinion of the drunken fellow's character," said Jack, "no one will dream for an instant we're supposed to be friends."

"They may guess we're near relations however, old fellow," I suggested.

Sir Francis guffawed.

"I wonder if Roger will be as witty after a few weeks teetotal diet?" he chuckled. "Mind you, Roger, you've got to play the game properly. No bringing a flask in your baggage or any humbug of that sort!"

"Don't you think an occasional relapse would add a touch of realism?" I suggested.

"Oh, if you can find liquor in the place, relapse by all means, so long as you don't give yourself away in your cups. But you've got to arrive without bottle, flask, or cup in your possession."

"It might be rather a happy touch, sir, if I were to go round sponging for drinks."

My uncle's earnestness was delightful. At this suggestion he put on his spectacles, and drew a paper from his pocket.

"Let me see," said he. "Here are a few directions given me by my own doctor, Sir James Macpherson. I had to give him some inkling of what I was after, but he is sworn to secrecy. Hum - No, Roger, you are trying religiously to cure yourself, and only very occasionally must the craving so far overcome you that you actually endeavour to secure alcoholic refreshment, as Sir James calls it. No promiscuous sponging, my boy, but a sponge now and then at considerable intervals might be advisable."

There was an interval of general conversation while one course succeeded another, and then Sir Francis resumed his instructions.

"With the help of a few tips from Sir James and my friends at the Admiralty, I have worked out the scheme very carefully, and I must beg you to get every detail most firmly into your head, Roger. Mind you, these poisonous fellows won't hesitate to stick a knife or a bullet into you, if they have the least suspicion of you. You know that as well as I do, and I don't want you to go and throw your life away, my boy."

I felt half inclined to smile, and half to do something more sentimental. He was such a dictatorial boss, and yet such a dear old fellow.

"I assure you I set more value on my life even than my friends do," I said.

" Well then get these instructions off by heart - and

don't forget one of them! I'll give you the paper to take away with you to-night, but meanwhile here are the principal points. In the first place, your name is Hobhouse - Thomas Sylvester Hobhouse."

I saw he was very pleased with this selection and asked tactfully,

"How did you manage to choose such excellent names, Uncle Francis?"

"I chose one name from the Red Book, another from the Peerage, and another from the Clerical Directory, so that one gets - er - a more natural and lifelike combination in that way; and yet avoids a real name. I think Thomas came from the Clerical directory - or was it the Peerage? Well, no matter, that's your name."

"And my occupation?"

"None: it saves prevarication and confusion. You've always been an idle dog, Roger, so I think 'a gentleman of no occupation' will be a sufficiently correct description. You are very well connected by the way."

"I am aware of it," I said, with a polite bow to my uncle and cousin.

But my uncle had grown too serious to appreciate such small change of conversation.

"Your relatives," he continued, "are in such high positions that they are entitled to ask Dr. Rendall not to make any indiscreet enquiries of his patient regarding his family, and also to appeal with success to a certain influential gentleman in the Government for permission to dump you in these prohibited islands. You , of course , know nothing of these steps. You have just recovered from a severe attack of *delirium tremens* - "

"My dear uncle!" I gasped, "is that Sir James's idea?"

"It is putting into definite terms what he obviously suggested. Under those circumstances you naturally know nothing of what your friends have been doing on your behalf. Dr. Rendall being informed of all these facts will of course refrain from putting awkward questions, the answers to which you might forget, even if I composed them for you."

"And how did my relatives hear of Dr. Rendall and the island of Ransay?" I enquired.

"I have thought over that point very carefully, Roger, and I think the best plan will be to take Sir James a little more into my confidence and get him to write a personal letter to Dr. Rendall. He will do it if I assure him it is for his country's sake, and his name will lull all suspicions."

My cousin and I thoroughly agreed with this last suggestion. In fact we found little fault with any part of the programme dictated to us, except the *delirium tremens*. Even Jack, though he itched to see me thus labelled, agreed with me that a less definite form of drunkenness would be safer, and finally Sir Francis decided to substitute "an alcoholic breakdown."

As for the rest of my instructions, I made one or two mental reservations. For instance, if Dr. Rendall himself was mixed up in the affair, he would scarcely refrain from putting questions to find out all about his guest; but I felt I need scarcely trouble my worthy uncle to compose the replies before hand.

I remember that little dinner very vividly. As it chanced it was my one glimpse of the old life of town and clubland and everything that goes with evening dress, seen just for that brief evening between months of mine-dodging and blizzard-facing in the North Sea followed by a hospital bed, and the lonely tempestuous isle of Ransay. The white napery, the gleam of glasses, the shaded electric lamps, the blazing fire, and the lofty soft-carpeted room left an impression that stayed with me for many a month to come. And in an easy chair after dinner, smoking the special cigar that my uncle conscientiously recommended and sipping the ancient cognac he advised, I should have been perfectly willing to listen to him had he suggested pushing me into a soft shore billet and letting some other poor devil grow a beard and hunt for spies in northern gales instead.

But he was not that sort of uncle.

"It's the chance of your life, Roger," he said. "By Gad, I wish I were young enough to take on the job myself. But you'll do the family credit I'm sure - if you only remember that this business requires discretion and caution quite as much as daring and resource!"

"Hear, hear!" said Jack. "Put that in your pipe and smoke it thoroughly, Roger."

"Whatever you do, don't trust one living soul in that place! The unlikeliest person may prove to be up to the neck in the business."

"Or only up to the ankles, yet they may give you away to some one else," added my cousin.

"And *à propos* of ankles," said my uncle, who was a confirmed bachelor, "Beware of women most of all! Never trust a secret to a woman, Roger - never!"

"There are none to confide in," I assured him, "except Miss Rendall - and she is one of the suspected; whatever Jack's gallantry may say."

"My gallantry is a thing of the past," said Jack, "I suspect everybody in that d - d place. And I'd advise you to do the same."

"Everybody!" echoed Sir Francis. "And confide in no one."

The evening came to an end at last, and with a sigh I left that comfortable smoking room. As I passed out into the hall, however, my uncle took my arm and made one brief but comforting speech in my ear.

"Don't worry about money matters, Roger, old fellow. Of course I'm paying the doctor's fee, and if you ever need anything more just let me know. If you bring this off - "

He did not finish his sentence but pressed my arm and gave me a nod and a smile.

J. Storer Clouston

III

THE ALCOHOLIC PATIENT

On a raw grey February morning Mr. Thomas Sylvester Hobhouse bade a polite farewell to the medical gentlemen who had escorted him thus far, and stepped aboard the little steamer sailing from a certain small and ancient port out into the northern isles of that archipelago. This medical escort was a typical instance of my uncle's relentless thoroughness. He was not in the secret, and so all the way from Euston to those remote islands I had to endure the ordeal of sitting under the eye of a conscientious middle-aged gentleman with a strong Yorkshire accent and but one idea in his head: - to keep in readiness to seize me at each station in case I leapt out of the carriage and headed for the refreshment rooms. We parted, I think, with equal relief on either side.

Under a heavy sky and a chilly wind we steamed through divers waterways, touched at divers islands, and shipped and unshipped many cattle. At last, when it had turned afternoon and the wind was beginning to feel wet as well as chilly, Thomas Sylvester stepped ashore on the modest pier at Ransay. Already he had noted from the deck his prospective host, pipe in mouth and hands in his knickerbocker pockets among a small knot of inhabitants, but to his relief there were no other familiar faces.

"Let me be firmly established as Mr. Hobhouse, the doctor's new paying guest, before they look at me too closely!" he said to himself.

In the doctor's blue eyes there was not a sign of recognition or suspicion. I noticed again his habit of glancing at one askance which had raised my ready suspicions last time we had met, but apart from that his greeting was cordial and pleasant enough.

"I've only got an open trap, Mr. Hobhouse," he said, "and it's a three mile drive. I hope you have got a warm coat."

Mr. Hobhouse, I may mention, was a gentleman with an extremely polite, nervously effusive manner, who always agreed with everybody and blinked a little as he looked at them with apologetic friendliness through his gold-rimmed glasses. Those who have seen that sprightly comedy "Heels Up" may perhaps remember the not unsuccessful character of Sir Douglas Jenkinson Bart (played by Mr. Roger Merton). Mr. Thomas Sylvester Hobhouse would have reminded them of Sir Douglas forcibly.

"Oh yes, doctor, a beautifully warm coat; you needn't worry about me at all. I shall be very comfortable - very comfortable indeed, thank you," Mr. Hobhouse assured him.

Dr. Rendall eyed his patient again, and there seemed to be a gleam of satisfaction in his glance, as though this were the kind of polite, acquiescent gentleman he liked.

There was a weary delay in getting my baggage out of the hold, and the February afternoon had grown greyer by the time we started in the doctor's pony trap. As the road was heavy with mud and covered with patches of loose metal every here and there, those three miles proved the longest I have ever driven. By this time the wind was sweeping clouds of fine rain into our faces, and seen through this driving vapour the island looked another place from the Ransay of summer time. The flowers were gone, and the corn, and even the greenness of the grass, which now was of a pale yellowish-olive hue; and I thought that a nakeder, more inhospitable looking spot surely man had never visited.

Under such circumstances we talked little; the doctor only making a remark now and then in a dutiful way, and Mr. Hobhouse effusively agreeing with him. That gentleman was quite content to postpone his enquiries until he had got a little warmer and drier, and at times he even felt acute anxiety lest the bleak house that loomed ahead, visible afar over the treeless country, was actually moving away from them. They seemed to approach it so slowly.

Evening was near at hand when Mr. Hobhouse entered his teetotal haven, and his effusiveness was quite sincere as he rubbed his hands over a blazing fire in the doctor's smoking room, and still sincerer when he faced an excellent high tea.

The conversation naturally turned on the war, and Thomas Sylvester showed an anxiety to learn his host's opinions and an enthusiastic agreement with each one of them that seemed to please the doctor. He became more and more talkative and genial , but though his guest mentally went through his words with a tooth-comb as he uttered them, he had to confess at the end of a chatty hour that the doctor exhibited neither any special knowledge of military and naval affairs, nor any lack of zeal for the cause of his country.

"No treason so far!" said Thomas to himself.

Then with what he flattered himself was the art which conceals art, Mr. Hobhouse brought the conversation round to the subject of the doctor himself and his household. He enthusiastically assured his host that each arrangement he mentioned was the best imaginable - from the doctor's being a bachelor to his having no hot water laid on in the bathroom but large cans brought when necessary. And presently he blinked more amiably than ever and enquired,

"And do you often have - er - guests, doctor; guests such as myself?"

The doctor's geniality seemed suddenly to contract a little.

"Occasionally," he said briefly.

"Quite so," agreed Mr. Hobhouse. "Too often would be a great nuisance. Occasionally - yes, yes, that must be much pleasanter. Just when you feel inclined; I see. And I hope you get decent fellows as a rule, doctor. It would be very unpleasant otherwise."

"It is," said Dr. Rendall with distinct emphasis.

"I trust *I* won't be a nuisance," said Mr. Hobhouse anxiously.

"Oh, no, no," said the doctor hurriedly, "I was thinking of - "

He broke off, and his amiable guest tactfully changed the subject. A little later, with what he hoped was equal tact, he returned to it again. Assuring the doctor of his anxiety to give no trouble, he said,

"I'll do just as the last fellow did. You just put me into his shoes, doctor, and then you'll always know where you are."

There was no doubt about the oddness of the glance which Dr. Rendall shot at his guest this time. His answer was a murmur that might have meant anything. Mr. Hobhouse innocently rattled on.

"I presume he fitted into your ways all right and so will I if you tell me first what - er - you did mention his name - or didn't you?"

"O'Brien," said the doctor.

"O'Brien?" repeated Mr. Hobhouse with a distinct air of distaste for so mild a gentleman.

The doctor looked at him quickly.

"Do you know him?" he asked sharply.

" Oh , no , no ! Oh dear me, no! It's only that I have a very foolish and very stupid prejudice against Irishmen - as I presume he was."

Mr. Hobhouse laughed pleasantly, and inwardly he laughed still more pleasantly, for his shot came off.

"So have I," agreed the doctor, and there was no doubt that he was in earnest.

Mr. Hobhouse decided that he had probed the matter sufficiently for the present, and with what he was now beginning to consider his usual tact he changed the subject.

Before they parted that night he could not resist one touch of art despite the counsels of Sir Francis.

"Before we go to bed, doctor," he said, with his most ingratiating smile, "do you think one little drop would do us any harm? I feel as though I might have a little cold coming on - "

But the doctor was shaking his head, kindly but firmly.

"Well, well, better not; I quite agree with you, doctor," gushed his guest. "Good-night, doctor. Good-night!"

"I wonder if the doctor ever had such a blinkin' ass in his house before!" said the amiable gentleman to himself as he shut his bed-room door behind him.

Looking at myself in the glass with a kind of chastened complacence, I decided that the man who could perceive in Mr. Hobhouse any reminiscence of the mysterious young stranger of six months ago would have a singularly piercing eye. At the same time it was a sobering experience to gaze at that black-bearded gentleman, with his hair parted in the middle and brushed low down over his forehead, and his foolish looking pince-nezs, and reflect that there was no artificial difference between him and the vanished Roger Merton save those eye-glasses and a little hair dye. That was my own face, and my own hair, and, I presumed, my own natural latent idiocy blinking behind those glasses. I turned away from the mirror with mingled feelings.

As the hour was not late (early to bed being part of the cure), I put on my dressing gown and sat down to smoke and chew the cud of my evening's conversation with Dr. Rendall. The more I saw of him, the more favourably on the whole the man impressed me. He was a gentleman and seemed a good fellow. Being a bachelor with outdoor tastes and an easygoing disposition, it was not at all impossible to understand his choosing the estate of his family to settle down on, isolated though it was. Certainly one could not honestly charge it against him as a suspicious circumstance.

By far the most interesting discovery was his obvious dislike to Mr. O'Brien. Not once but several times he had shown it in the course of our talk. He conveyed the suggestion moreover that the man had oppressed him in some way and that it was a relief to have got rid of him. In view of the fact that he had been so anxious to secure another resident patient, this seemed a little odd, and a theory began to take shape in my mind. Supposing O'Brien had in some way induced the doctor unwillingly to abet a treasonable scheme, that would account for his feelings very well, especially looking to O'Brien's unpleasing personality. But on the other hand, events had made it clear that treason was going on without O'Brien, so how could the doctor have got clear of it? And if he were still in it, this theory of his relations to his late patient was manifestly weak.

"To bed!" said Thomas Sylvester to himself, after an hour of these reflections. "You are theorizing too soon."

In the morning he was up betimes and downstairs a good ten minutes before he knew the doctor was likely to appear. Into the smoking room he went, shut the door carefully behind him, and made for the window. A grey and windy prospect met his eyes, but they scarcely glanced at it. Mr. Hobhouse had something else to think of. Twice or thrice he pulled the blind up and down, and minutely examined the string and the little brass pulley.

"That blind certainly does not come down at a touch," he said to himself, "and there is not a sign of its having been repaired within the last few years. Therefore it did not drop accidentally six months ago."

IV

THE TEST

That afternoon, as the weather had cleared somewhat, Dr. Rendall proposed walking over to his cousin's house and presenting Mr. Hobhouse to the laird and his daughter. This ordeal had to be undergone sooner or later, so I decided I had better fall in with his suggestion and get it over at once. Besides, it was an obvious part of my programme to make a great deal of outdoor exercise a principal feature of Mr. Hobhouse's cure, and I felt bound to agree at once with any proposal to take a walk. We had taken the precaution, by the way, of telling the doctor beforehand of my limp (caused by a motoring accident when I was at the wheel in a condition I should not have been in) and assuring him that the surgeon encouraged exercise to complete the cure. So off we set for the "big house."

On the way the doctor gave his guest a certain amount of general information concerning the people they were going to meet, but as Mr. Hobhouse happened to know it already, it need not be chronicled here.

As the pair approached the weather beaten old mansion, looking now in its true setting against the wintry sky, Thomas Sylvester became acutely conscious of the return of a familiar sensation. It was, in fact, precisely the sensation which one Roger Merton had enjoyed when waiting for his cue to step from dim obscurity into the flare of the footlights on the first night of a new drama. Would his old acquaintances accept Mr. Hobhouse without question as an entire stranger? If he spied so much as one suspicious questioning glance, his whole scheme was exploded.

We were shown into the drawing room, and to my great relief Mr. Rendall was the first to appear, for I felt I could stand the scrutiny of Jean's bright eyes a deal more readily if I had once got into the swing of talk with her father. In his eye there was certainly no trace of question. With his dry and formidable courtesy he greeted Mr. Hobhouse and in a minute or two they were talking away in that friendly fashion which Mr. Hobhouse was pleased to notice people fell into very readily with him. And small wonder, for the creature was so grossly affable, and (if I say it myself) so infernally plausible.

His great hobby, it appeared, was antiquarian research, and though he let slip a few remarks that showed he was well versed in his subject, his role, as usual, was that of the flatteringly eager enquirer. Needless to say, his learning had been acquired by diligent application within the last week, and that it had a very definite object behind it. The laird had but a smattering of the subject, but being an intelligent, well-read man, he was quite able to discuss Mr. Hobhouse's favourite pursuit, so that when his daughter entered the room she found herself in an atmosphere as little reminiscent of the mysterious stranger as it was possible to create in the time.

All the same, it was an anxious moment when Jean's eyes first fell upon him, and he heaved a deep sigh of relief when he saw not a spark of recognition in them. On his part, Thomas Sylvester was scrupulously careful to avoid the least resemblance to the conduct of the mysterious Merton, even in the smallest point. There was no assurance, no tribute of attention and consciousness of her presence, such as a girl as charming as Miss Rendall has the right to expect from every man with an eye in his head; and which I must confess the mysterious stranger used to pay her, for all her dislike to him. Mr. Hobhouse of course was dreadfully polite, but seemed a little shy of the sex, and after a few commonplaces on either side, she turned to her cousin and he to his host.

Tea was brought in, and the party chatted away as amicably as any party of four in the kingdom. Thomas had found his tea party legs by this time and quite enjoyed the situation. Mr. Rendall impressed him much more favourably than he had impressed Roger Merton. The grimness seemed to fall off the man when one got him going in talk and a vein of kindliness opened instead.

"I'm dashed if there seems to be anything suspicious in anybody this time!" said Mr. Hobhouse to himself rather disconsolately.

He had hardly made this reflection when he happened to glance at Jean. This as a matter of fact had happened several times previously. For one thing she was looking a picture, and for another the alcoholic visitor liked to reassure himself at intervals that she was still without shadow of suspicion. And each time he had felt perfectly reassured.

But this time he was conscious of a sudden thrill of certainty that Miss Rendall had been covertly studying him, and that now (though her eyes turned away instantly) she had some new food for thought. Instantly he asked for another cup of tea and blinked at her benignantly as their eyes met. Did he actually read in hers confirmation of his first instinctive feeling, or was it only a too quick imagination? Mr. Hobhouse wondered very seriously.

Thereafter for some little time, as he talked with her father, he was acutely aware that both she and the doctor were very silent, and when now and then he glanced at her, she seemed to be thinking rather than listening. And then, just as he was beginning to grow a trifle uneasy, this phase seemed to pass away and the next time he looked at her she met his glance with a faint smile. In fact she had smiled several times before the doctor and his patient took their departure, and as they shook hands at the end Thomas Sylvester was agreeably conscious of the kindest look she had ever favoured him with. And finally when her father hoped they might see their new acquaintance soon again, she joined him in hoping, both with her words, and (it seemed to him) her eyes.

During the first part of their walk home, Mr. Hobhouse was very silent. Going back over their call, while everything was fresh in his memory, he had to confess that his prejudices against Mr. Rendall were ready to vanish altogether if he were ready to let them. In fact the grim ironic Mr. Rendall conversing with the suspicious stranger was an entirely different person from the friendly Mr. Rendall who conversed with the innocent-looking Thomas Sylvester Hobhouse. On the face of it this was obviously to be explained by his suspicions of the stranger. But of what did he suspect him? Of being a German spy, as he professed? Or of being what he was? That was the whole point, and it seemed to me that getting him arrested and removed was equally consistent with either alternative.

But what of his daughter, that slim, dangerously dainty piece of mystery? Were her two changes of attitude in the course of this afternoon mere mirages seen by an eye disordered by suspicion? They might be, but Mr. Hobhouse was prepared to stake his davy that they were real. And what then did they imply? Surely not that she suspected the truth. He could not read them into that. That she was simply a coquette and for want of more amusing game (such for instance as Mr. O'Brien) was prepared to have a little flirtation with his successor? This was, somehow or other, not a very agreeable solution, but I began to suspect it might be the true one. In any case she was a puzzling factor, and the best course of action seemed to me to be to avoid her society in the meanwhile, and to keep my eyes wide open for possible trouble. I hardly thought there would be trouble, but it were well to be on the lookout.

This being decided, the amiable Mr. Hobhouse started conversation with the doctor, and gradually by gentle and circuitous methods led the talk, via the war in general, to the part in the war played by these islands, and to any interesting events that might have happened in them. He was heading in his devious way for the visit of the suspicious stranger, but at this point the doctor brought him in of his own accord.

"We had one most extraordinary thing happen in this place," said he. "Nobody has got to the bottom of it yet."

"Really!" cried Mr. Hobhouse. "How very interesting! What was it?"

"Well," said the doctor, "one morning when I had that fellow O'Brien staying with me, a young man walked into my house under the impression - so he said - that it was my cousin's. Whether he told the truth or not I've often wondered since. He had no cap, was buttoned up in an oilskin coat (though I may say it was a fine morning) and talked with a distinct foreign accent. I could swear it was German, but O'Brien, who contradicted everything, stuck to it it was Russian. A lot he knew about Russian! He was only in the house about five minutes , for when he discovered his mistake - or what he said was his mistake - he went off. And that is all I saw of him personally."

"But did he go to Mr. Rendall's then?"

The doctor nodded.

"He turned up there and spent two or three nights in the house. The chap had the impudence of the devil. He said he had been landed from one of our own cruisers and didn't want to be recognised as an officer, so would they be kind enough to lend him a coat and let him lock his uniform coat up in a drawer! He was in his oilskin all this time, you must remember. A day or two later my cousins grew suspicious and opened that drawer. What do you think they found?"

"Maps!" guessed Mr. Hobhouse.

"Nothing at all! He had never had a uniform coat. They promptly wired to the Naval Authorities, locked him in his room meanwhile, and when Commander Whiteclett appeared he arrested him and took him off."

"And who was he?"

The doctor turned to his guest with an expression of considerable indignation.

"The damned secrecy of these navy people is past belief! Do you know that not even my cousins who caught the man for them were ever told a single word about him! Whiteclett took him straight off to his drifter without so much as saying good-bye - much less thank you - to my cousin Philip, and that was the last of it!"

"Then you never learned who the fellow was?"

"He gave his name as Merton - George or was it Roger? - Merton. But you can believe as much of that as you like."

"And did he land from a cruiser?"

"Not likely! But nobody was ever told how he did land. They found what they said was a parachute, but it's my belief that was either a blind or it was really some kind of collapsible boat. I never saw the thing myself, and O'Brien, who did see it, having heard somebody say it was a parachute, of course swore it was not."

"And did the man do nothing while he was on the island?"

"God knows what he may not have done! Naturally he told nobody what he was after, and no one actually saw him doing anything, but there are plenty of stories."

"What kind of stories?"

"Oh, the usual kind, that he was seen flashing lights on the shore and carrying petrol tins. But you can believe as much of them as you like."

"And have your cousins no theory? They apparently saw a good deal of him."

"My cousin Philip says frankly he is absolutely beaten by the whole performance. Jean - well girls are rum things."

"What are Miss Rendall's views then?" I enquired.

"She is generally quick enough at guessing, and as fond of gossip as most of her sex, but for some reason she keeps very quiet about it. It's my belief she knows something. In fact I shouldn't be surprised if Whiteclett had told her a little and sworn her to secrecy. Men do tell women things sometimes, as I daresay you have noticed for yourself, Mr. Hobhouse."

"What a very strange story!" murmured Mr. Hobhouse.

So this was the tale of my escapade as it was told in Ransay. The doctor's manner of telling it was the best guarantee of his own good faith I could wish, and I was ready now to dismiss the blind incident as a misleading trifle. But O'Brien seemed to have gone out of his way to throw doubt on every point raised, - and curiously enough to have always offered a wrong solution. It might be sheer contrariness, but it stuck me as odd. As to Miss Jean's silence, what did that mean? I resolved to keep my eyes very wide open indeed.

V

WAITING

By a fortunate chance Dr. Rendall was no expert in antiquarian matters, and yet had sufficient respect for those who were to give them every encouragement and make all allowances for any irregularity in their hours caused thereby. Mr. Hobhouse possessed several very learned looking volumes, such as "The Early Christian Monuments of Scotland," "The Windy Isles in Early Celtic Times," "Ecclesiological Notes on Some of the Islands of Scotland," and other tomes of that nature, and from these he could quote whole paragraphs without so much as pausing for breath (in fact he dared not pause, lest he forget). Mr. Hobhouse moreover talked in his garrulous way of adding his own modest contribution to this literature in the shape of a monograph on the antiquities of Ransay.

With this end in view it was therefore very natural that he should spend much of his time rambling over the island, particularly along the coasts, where he declared the early monuments he was especially interested in were mostly to be found, and should even at times be detained by his enthusiasm till darkness had fallen. It was also very natural that he should wish to consult all the most ancient inhabitants, and should in consequence seek out and interview every native over

J. Storer Clouston

sixty years of age. In short this hobby not only gave this enthusiastic gentleman a sound pretext for being in the most out of the way places at the most unlikely hours, but also for inspecting narrowly with his own eyes each white bearded patriarch who might, or might not, have worn six months ago a pair of tinted spectacles; which - to descend slightly in the literary scale - accounts for the milk in the cocoanut.

All this of course was not only perceived by his guardian medical attendant, but blessed with his strong approval, for nothing counteracts the taste for liquor so effectually as another hobby. But what Thomas Sylvester devoutly prayed the doctor did not see was his patient slipping out of his window in the small hours of the morning, and from the roof of an out-house just below, examining the shore through a night glass. In February and March weather this was far too uncomfortable to last long or to be repeated every night, and the shore was too far away to make it very effective. Still, he did think he noticed a glimmer once or twice, and each time his antiquarian expedition next day included certain artless enquiries which might have thrown some light on the matter had the answers been satisfactory. As a matter of fact, however, they never were, and the extraordinary appearance of interest with which the effusive gentleman listened to useless information reflected more credit on his resolution than any one will ever realise.

I may add that the professional watchers in the island were not of course in the secret of Mr. Hobhouse's identity, and therefore could not report to him directly anything they might see or suspect. But if they did see or suspect anything he would very quickly be informed through another source. However Commander

Whiteclett based no great hopes on the possibility of catching our wily enemy out by means of a palpable man in uniform, and Mr. H. had been instructed to act exactly as though he were alone on the job.

One of his earliest expeditions was made to the site of a prehistoric building in the near vicinity of the Scollays' farm. At least there was a grassy knoll visible which Mr. H.'s expert eye at once pronounced to be worthy of very careful inspection, and in order to confirm his theories he decided to visit the farm to make enquiry as to any possible traditions regarding it.

He passed round the knoll with this purpose, to discover that he was no longer meditating alone. A familiar figure confronted him, with dark staring eyes, gaping mouth, and stubby beard; my old friend Jock. For a moment there returned that feeling of stage fright. Next to the Rendalls, the Scollay household, and particularly Jock, had seen and conversed most often with the mysterious Merton. Jock was only an idiot, but where reason is lacking instinct is apt to be strong, and instinct might distinguish an old acquaintance through all my disguise. Anyhow, rightly or wrongly, I felt that this was another delicate moment.

"Good-day, my good fellow. Good-day to you!" said the friendly Mr. Hobhouse. "A little better weather to-day!"

The surprise of the affable gentleman at getting only a grunt in reply, his air of gradual comprehension, and then of friendly sympathy, were acted for all they were worth. And to my vast relief, Jock showed no glimmer of recognition of the young man with the revolver.

"Do you know who lives at that farm?" enquired Mr. Hobhouse speaking very distinctly. "Tolly, you say? Oh, jolly? Yes, very jolly! Ha, ha! Good-bye, my lad, good-bye to you!"

Jock's hoot of laughter was answered by Mr. Hobhouse's giggle, and they set off down to the farm, the antiquary in front limping rather more markedly than usual, and the idiot rambling behind.

The visit to the Scollays was a distinct success, so far as establishing the personality of Mr. Thomas Sylvester Hobhouse went. At first they looked at him with an obvious suspicion and replied to his questions with a reticence that gave him a few uneasy moments. But in ten minutes his indefatigable friendliness had conquered the household and he knew that he was safe to visit that knoll whenever the fancy took him. Peter senior told him a long story about the fairies who were seen dancing round the knoll in his father's time, and though his family were evidently a little distressed by his reference to anything so unfashionable, and Jock hooted several times, their visitor exhibited the liveliest interest and put the tale religiously down in his note book.

This was all that could be done at the moment; the establishment of a perfectly harmless reputation and of a natural reason for visiting that particular place at odd times. Mr. Hobhouse obtained permission to do a little digging there if he desired it, and parted with the family on the best of terms.

"Slow work!" he said to himself as he struck out for home, with his limp rapidly vanishing. "But what the devil else can one do ? What is there definite to take hold of?"

That was the baffling feature of the business. As my cousin said, such scent as there was had grown cold by this time, and one had to begin at the beginning again. And so far there seemed to be no beginning. The detectives of fiction might have found some clue to start a train of logical and inevitable reasoning that led straight to the criminal, but the detective of fact had utterly failed, and the brilliant young amateur of fact was likewise completely at sea.

What good for instance had my visit to the Scollays done? I asked myself. If they were innocent I had wasted my time. If they were guilty, what had I discovered to bring it home to them? Absolutely nothing! And the same with each inhabitant of that island whom I had seen. Some cunning and powerful organisation was certainly at work, to the detriment of my country, but the only point I had scored against them, was that I had got into the place without their recognising me. At least I presumed I had or I should scarcely still be alive to tell the tale - unless they had grown either more merciful or more timid since I was here last. And their continued immunity would scarcely be likely to produce either of those effects.

The only specific thing I could think of looking for was the old man with the tinted spectacles. So far I was well on the way to proving one thing about him, and that the least satisfactory thing I could prove. Apparently Bolton was right and no such person existed. Therefore I was as far off catching him as ever, and had merely the added certainty that my enemies were extremely resourceful and spared no trouble to make sure of things when in doubt.

However, I meant to go on looking till I had exhausted all the old men in the place. I was about half way through them by this time, so far as I could calculate.

Thus the winter days passed, growing longer but no warmer and no finer. One would have had early touches of spring by this time in the South, but here it was still winter undiluted. The violence and frequency of the winds was amazing. Indeed I seldom remember having less than a stiff breeze, and every now and then a full tearing howling gale would scour the bare low-lying island till it seemed as if even the houses could scarcely stand up to it much longer, while the sea would be one bewildering chaos of breaking and subsiding crests, white against the leaden furrows, surging on till they smashed into a continuous line of foam along our iron coast.

How the wind howled and whistled round that melancholy mansion of the doctor's! I forget who had built it, or why; some land agent or factor, I think, who had once lived on the estate, but I know I frequently cursed him. It stood up just high enough to catch the full force of every blast that blew, and not quite high enough to get a really fine view. There was too much bleak foreground, so that one got no value from the site whatever so far as I could see. And, lord, it was draughty!

My only company was the doctor, and he was out most of the day. Even at nights I began to find him a curiously moody companion. There were moments when my suspicions revived again; he used to glance at me furtively, leave the room mysteriously for half an hour at a time, and do little more than grunt when he was spoken to. And then next day he would be such a pleasant, sensible, downright sort of fellow that I could only remember his simple telling of the tale of my own visit, and dismiss him from my calculations.

And so life went on for some three weeks uneventfully enough for a desperate and disguised adventurer. I received several letters from my uncle, and I was thankful it had been arranged I should not answer them. The dear man had evidently such a twopenny-coloured conception of the hazardous life I was leading that a truthful recital of my adventures might have brought him down in person to stir things up. But there was nothing to stir; I could only wait.

VI

THE SPECTACLED MAN

It was, I remember, on a rare day of bright, still, frosty weather, that Mr. Hobhouse returned a little late for the doctor's mid-day dinner. The garrulous creature was looking thoughtful and, as it were, subdued; wanting a dram, no doubt, thought any who chanced to spy him in this unusual condition. But as he opened the front door he became his foolish self instantaneously. The sound of a strange voice had reached him distinctly.

"Let me introduce Captain Whiteclett - Mr. Hobhouse," said the doctor,

He and the stranger had already begun dinner, and Commander Whiteclett rose and bowed politely. Mr. Hobhouse bowed still more politely and having the advantage of being at the doctor's back for the moment, was able to embellish his low obeisance with several curious facial expressions. The Commander at the same moment was attacked with a sharp bout of coughing, but presently recovering, the meal proceeded very pleasantly.

It appeared that Commander Whiteclett was visiting the island in the course of a tour of inspection, and having some acquaintance with the doctor had dropped in for lunch. He seemed pleased to meet Mr. Hobhouse and was as affable as naval officers always are, though every now and then it might have been noticed by a very close observer that after meeting that gentleman's eye, he showed a tendency to stare suddenly out of the window for several moments. Mr. Hobhouse on his part was in his most gushing humour, and in fact chatted almost continuously through the meal.

As they passed out of the dining room ahead of the doctor, the two guests exchanged a whisper, and about quarter of an hour later Mr. Hobhouse declared that he must set forth and resume his antiquarian researches, and effusively bade the Commander good-bye. Thereupon the Commander said he also must be off and wondered in which direction his fellow guest was walking. It chanced that they were both going the same way and so they departed together.

"Well, you ridiculous looking dipsomaniac, how do you like water for dinner?" enquired the Commander when they were safely out of earshot.

"It lies cold on the tummy," said I, "and if you've brought a flask, Jack - "

"I have," said my cousin, "but wait a bit till there are no witnesses. And by the way, old chap, I must tell you that you're a d - d good actor."

"My photograph has appeared in the *Tatler*" I confessed.

"And what news?" he asked.

" Up till this morning I should have said 'none.' My

dear Jack, it has been the most hopelessly baffling business you can possibly imagine. I think I am quite a success as an alcoholic patient, and also accepted by this time as the typical harmless antiquary. So I am able to wander all over the place and talk to everybody, but there has been nothing to take hold of! I have seen no sign of anything happening - " I caught his eye and asked quickly, "Has anything happened?"

He nodded.

"Signalling night before last and a submarine seen yesterday that we suspect of having been here."

"Under my nose!" I groaned. "A fat lot of good I am!"

"My dear chap, you can't possibly watch the whole coast all night and every night. This time the signals were seen from the sea as a matter of fact. But you can note the night, and also the hour, which was 2:45 a.m., G.M.T., as near as I can make out from the report. By the way, you had better set your watch by mine now while we remember. Possibly you may be able to discover who was out at that hour night before last."

"I may, but it's a thousand to one against it. Give me a thousand such chances, and I'll get him! That's just about how it seems to work out so far."

"Haven't you got any new ideas?"

"Without new evidence, what new ideas can one get? And I only got my first piece of evidence this morning. In fact, I haven't had time to think it over yet."

"Let's hear it," said my cousin keenly.

"I have been on the track of that old boy with spectacles, as being the only definite thing to look for so far. I did what Bolton did - went to see every old man in the place, and this morning I polished off the last of them and came to the same conclusion as he did. There is no such old gentleman on the island. But there *was* one, for a short time one morning; and he was a fake like Thomas Sylvester Hobhouse; and this morning I've heard of some one else who saw him!"

"By Gad!" exclaimed my cousin. "That sounds like the beginning of business."

"Only the beginning, I'm afraid. This morning I interview my last old man - to find of course he wasn't the fellow I was after. I interviewed him on the usual subject - ancient traditions of the island, and from that we passed on to the latest tradition, the legend of the mysterious visitor last August. He told me all about it, with many embellishments. However he was shrewd enough not to believe all he heard, and to show me what absurd stories are put about, he informed me that his own small grand-daughter, aged six, had declared that she had seen the mysterious visitor, only she described him as having a white beard and funny spectacles. I asked him exactly where this phenomenon had been observed, and by Jingo, Jack, it was at the very place I met him; only when she saw him he had left the road and was hurrying down to the sea. She described him as running, which finally demolished her reputation for truthfulness, for as her grandfather observed, men of his age don't run. But that was my friend right enough!"

"Heading for the sea?"

"For the beach, I take it. You see you can pop over the edge almost anywhere along that shore, and get out of sight among the rocks in a moment. I presume he squatted down there, pocketed his spectacles and beard, took off his disreputable overcoat, and either hid it or possibly pinned up the skirts and put it on under his other coat, and walked off looking like - well, that's the rub, what did he look like then? And that's just where I seem no forrader."

"Still, this is something."

"Yes, and I suppose we ought to deduce something more from the episode. I've already concluded that the high piping voice he used might well have concealed an accent, and I've also decided from what I've heard of the local language since that he hadn't the native intonation."

"And he headed for the beach," added my cousin. "Therefore he certainly did not come from any house in the near neighbourhood."

"That puts the doctor's house out of court, if you're right. But he may possibly have thought it better not to do his dressing up at home."

"I see you've still got you knife into O'Brien!" laughed my cousin. "But I think my notion is the likeliest - "

He broke off suddenly and we instinctively moved a pace further apart. A figure had appeared round a turn of the road just ahead of us, a trim, dainty figure, delightful to see in such a place, but a little disconcerting to see so suddenly and so close to us. It was Jean Rendall, looking her best, but not, it seemed to me, quite in the right place.

Had she noticed anything? There was not a sign of it in her greeting. She gave us both one of her quick smiles, and as Jack pulled up to speak to her, she stopped too, and in talking to him, I noticed afresh how full of expression those neatly chiselled, rather petite, features became when she talked, and what a charming little air of knowing her way about the world she had. Young though she was, I could see in her very clearly either a valuable friend or a dangerous enemy - and what an easy girl to fall in love with, had circumstances been very different!

Jack explained in a very natural off-hand manner how he came to be in Mr. Hobhouse's company, and Mr. Hobhouse corroborated his statement in his own effusive way. And then as we parted, she threw her smile full on that gentleman, and asked,

"Why haven't you been to see us again, Mr. Hobhouse? Do come to tea one day!"

Mr. Hobhouse gabbled a polite but slightly, evasive reply, and we walked on.

"Do you mean to say," demanded my cousin, "that you have only been to see this delectable lady once?"

"That's all," I admitted.

"What's the reason? It isn't very like our methods, Roger."

"It isn't," I admitted again. "But then you see what with pestilential weather and all these antiquarian visits to pay, my available time has been pretty well occupied."

"But that house is one to keep a particular eye on."

"That house has got a pair of particularly bright eyes in it. On my one visit there I felt a little too like walking on the edge of a precipice to wish to repeat the experience often. If that girl suspects me, Jack, and *if* she isn't the right sort, we are dished."

"Oh, dash it. I can't believe she's mixed up in this business!" he declared. "Of course one mustn't trust anybody; still, that doesn't prevent your going to tea with her. In fact what you really ought to be doing is making love to her - so long as you keep your head."

"I am handicapped," I pointed out, "by drunken habits, a beard, and Mother Beagle's Beautiful Black Dye. No, Jack, I do not see orange blossom this trip."

"Apart from these romantic dreams," persisted my cousin, "she is far more likely to be inquisitive about you if you never go near the house. In fact I could see it in her eye to-day."

"Well," I said, "I'll call to-morrow and dispel her interest in me."

Since my talk with the doctor, his theory about Jean Rendall had crossed my mind occasionally, and improbable as it was, I thought I might as well test it.

"By the way," I asked, "did you by any chance ever speak to Miss Rendall about my last visit to the island?"

His look of surprise was a sufficient answer in itself.

"Speak to her of your adventure? Not a word at any time! Why?"

"The doctor has an idea that she knows more than she says, and that you may have told her something."

"Rubbish!"

"I knew it was," I assured him.

And so that possibility was finally eliminated.

We thought it wiser that our ways should part some little distance from the pier.

"Good-luck, old chap," said he, shaking my hand. "Keep playing the game you're at and don't worry about trying to keep a lookout at nights. That's being done already, and though I don't believe the fellows are much use - not with such crafty devils against them - you can't do anything to help 'em. Getting out at night is too risky, and you're too far away at the house. Your game is to work it from the other end. Sooner or later they are absolutely bound to give you a clue."

His spirit and my little discovery of the morning sent me back in a distinctly more hopeful mood.

VII

A REMINISCENCE

Next day I set out in the early afternoon to pay my call. The fine weather still held, bright sunshine with a nip in the air and the road underfoot firm with frost, and I strode along in a wonderfully confident mood, all things considered. For to tell the truth, I had been funking this visit. Instinctively I did not trust myself with Miss Jean Rendall. If she had any suspicions and if she turned on to me the art of her sex and the charms of her particular self, I was well aware that Thomas Sylvester would have a bad time of it. In fact I really dared not answer for the fellow's nerve. He being both critical and susceptible, a girl with Jean's distinctive aroma was dangerous company with a job of this kind on hand. And playing the whisky-enfeebled fool in a dirty black beard ceased entirely to amuse me when the other party was Miss Rendall. However, this morning Mr. Hobhouse felt braver, and stepped out briskly, resolved to do his bit.

As he approached the house, the front door opened and the very lady herself appeared. She carried a stick and was evidently setting forth on a walk.

"This is very nice of you to come so soon, Mr. Hobhouse , " she said. "I am glad I hadn't gone further before you appeared."

"Oh, but don't let me stop you, Miss Rendall," said Mr. Hobhouse anxiously. "Really, I can't allow it; no, no, really not. You mustn't turn back, indeed you mustn't! Perhaps I shall find Mr. Rendall at home."

"I was only going for a walk to nowhere in particular." She looked at him with an irresistible mixture of coyness and frankness and suggested, "Would you care to come for a little walk too? It's far too early for tea."

What could the poor gentleman do? He gushed over the suggestion of course, and accepted it.

"I was going to walk down to the shore," she said. "Will that suit you?"

Mr. Hobhouse assured her that anywhere would suit him; he had no choice at all: anywhere, everywhere, nowhere would be all the same to him.

As they walked side by side down towards the sea, he was suddenly struck with the sense of being in a familiar situation, of a repetition of something that had happened before. And then he realised that this was actually the walk that the same girl and a young man Merton had taken on a memorable August night. He noted through his glasses the very wall behind which he had lit his pipe when the flare of his match revealed the butt end of a pistol, and presently they were following the same winding way above the beach.

This did not serve to make the playing of his part any the easier. It filled him in fact with a continual fear of giving himself away by doing something he had done before. It was really a most irrational fear; but there it was. Under the circumstances his sustained babble and blink were distinctly creditable.

But what gave him a more excusable cause for apprehension was Miss Rendall's own attitude. That there was something on her mind, something behind her words, he felt morally certain. She spoke in the most natural way and on the most commonplace topics, but there were frequent silences and it was during those he felt that without looking directly at him, she was watching him. And once or twice he got it into his head that she was a little puzzled and uncertain, though whether it was about what to think or what to do, he had no conception. He told himself that all this was only his own morbid imagination. Still, it made that walk an uncomfortable ordeal and seldom did actor have to work harder to keep his end up.

Luckily however the man had the virtue of impudence and not only did he manage to entertain the lady with a garrulous account of his antiquarian researches (reasoning acutely that women are seldom experts in such matters), but he even ventured to broach a delicate subject for his own ends.

"The gentleman who - er - resided with Dr. Rendall last summer was not, I believe, very interested in antiquities," he observed. "Did you know him, Miss Rendall? Mr. O'Brien was his name, I believe."

"Yes," she said, "I knew Mr. O'Brien."

There was certainly no trace of any feeling, whether of like or dislike, in her voice.

"Not a very pleasant fellow, I believe," Mr. Hobhouse went on. "At least I should judge not; I should gather not. But I trust he wasn't a friend of yours, Miss Rendall?"

"Not a particular friend. But why do you think he was unpleasant?"

"Oh, only from Dr. Rendall's references to him - only from that, I assure you," said Mr. Hobhouse with propitiating eagerness.

"Really?" said she, her eyes opening.

There was no doubt that this information genuinely surprised her.

"I thought they seemed great friends," she added.

"Oh, they may have been - they may have been. I may be doing Mr. O'Brien an injustice. Possibly I misunderstood your relative - quite possibly."

She was silent for a little while after this, and Mr. Hobhouse too ceased chatting. He was eyeing the shore line very curiously and trying to piece together his recollections of it.

"I think perhaps we have gone far enough now," said she, and for a minute or two they stood still; and a very distinct sense of being in a familiar situation was borne in upon her companion.

And then all at once she exclaimed,

"Do you hear anything?"

I started and stared at her. For the moment I had ceased to be Mr. Hobhouse, so straight had I been carried back to that night six months ago. Those were her very words, and if I were not much mistaken this was the very place. I nearly answered as I had answered before, but was just able to check myself. And then she broke the spell by laughing.

"It's only the sea! But it sounded so funny and hollow."

There was indeed a low gurgle just audible, as if the waves were breaking into some cave. It struck me that she must have singularly sharp ears to have noticed it. We stood there for a minute or two longer, and then she asked,

"Do you see any ancient remains, Mr. Hobhouse?"

It was not in fact ancient remains that the eye glasses were looking at, but I jumped at the chance of making sure of my bearings, and with an appearance of great eagerness told her that there seemed to be something decidedly interesting in the appearance of the rocks at that place.

"I can wait for a moment if you'd like to look at them nearer," she said.

"This is luck!" I said to myself as I scrambled down. "I believe I've found the actual place."

A few minutes exploration left no doubt in my mind. I found the very cliff face under which I had been decoyed and was able to clear up one point. A man above could easily have struck at me with some implement, say, six feet long. I shut my eyes and pictured that curved mystery, and then in a flash I had it: a scythe blade tied to a pole! If I could find a scythe blade fastened to a pole, or a blade and pole separate, I should not be far off the end of my quest. The next moment I smiled at my own optimism when I realised what a house to house hunt that would imply. Still, I saw a fresh possibility and came back silently thanking my guide.

Conversation was rather easier coming back, perhaps because I felt in higher spirits and could play my absurd part with more gusto. Still, the girl remained a little disquieting. She was now in a very smiling and friendly mood, and a man who blinked through gold rimmed glasses and giggled through a dyed beard ought to have felt exceedingly flattered. But now I was saying to myself that for a girl of fastidious taste she was really too nice to such a fellow. And then I remembered that O'Brien had a black beard too, and the thought struck me,

"Can she have such pleasant recollections of black beards that I am providing her with reminiscent romance?"

I think it was just as this idea occurred to me that she roused me very sharply from my meditations.

"I suppose you have heard of the mysterious man who appeared here last summer?" she enquired.

It took Mr. Hobhouse all this time to adjust himself to this question, but I think he managed it not unsuccessfully.

" The - ah? Oh , yes , oh, yes. The doctor told me the

story. Most mysterious - most mysterious! What do you make of it yourself, Miss Rendall?"

"Did the doctor tell you that I once walked with him along this very shore? It was at night too, and he was armed with a pistol!"

A single stare of astonishment was fortunately able to cover two emotions. My own was expressed in the thought, "What the devil is she driving at now?" Mr. Hobhouse's was expressed otherwise.

"You don't say so! God bless me; what a risk to run! He didn't - er - shoot at you, I hope?"

"No," she said, "he seemed pretty harmless."

"Ah, but you shouldn't run such risks, my dear young lady; you really shouldn't! Now I remember a young lady whom I used to know - " And thereupon Mr. Hobhouse launched into an improbable anecdote which tried his inventive powers considerably. However, he was able to make it, and the comments thereupon lasted till they were back at the house.

The fact was that my hardihood was not quite sufficient to stand a conversation about my own self behind my own back. It might have been amusing, and it might have been instructive, but it would certainly have been embarrassing. However the incident served to reassure me that whatever she suspected me of (and I could not get that sense of being watched out of my head), it was not the correct suspicion. Had she guessed the truth I could see no point at all in her reminiscence of the mysterious stranger, unless it were sheer pointless mischief, and she did not seem a pointless lady. Besides, when I glanced at myself in the drawing room mirror, I said to myself, "Who could possibly guess!"

After that walk, tea and a talk with her father were unexciting episodes. She kept very much in the background, but when we parted I seemed to note again that flicker of a very alluring smile.

"Can it be that she has a morbid taste for inebriates?" I wondered. "One has heard of women with curiously diseased fancies. Or perhaps she has simply a passion for reforming them. One of those smiles for every sober hour would be a distinct inducement to behave!"

But this was not business and as I walked home I turned my thoughts sternly to that scythe blade.

J. Storer Clouston

VIII

H.M.S. *Uruguay*

As I neared my bleak sanatorium I said to myself,

"If only something would happen!"

Week after week spent within those walls or in wandering over this limited space of muddy roads and sodden fields, with nothing to show for it, was an unexhilarating prospect. Perhaps the recollection of the comfortable house and the pleasant company I had just left accentuated this feeling, and the swift disappearance of our glimpse of crispness and sunshine did nothing to raise the heart. In that low-lying isle one got the most extraordinary views of the weather and could see storms approaching when they were still leagues away, and portents of rain or wind hours ahead of their coming. This evening the frost had vanished, the sun was sinking into a grey-blue bank, little filaments of wind clouds were reaching all over the sky, and a stiff chilly breeze was already blowing in from the sea.

"We are going to have a change," I thought.

And we were indeed going to have a change; and of more than weather. Those storm clouds were blowing up the something I wanted to happen, though how promptly would I have changed my wish had I but guessed! But Fate had loosed that nor'west gale and there was no stopping the order of things now.

In the night I remember waking once or twice to hear the wind shouting down the chimney, and to feel very snug in bed. When I got up it was still blowing a full gale, and looking out of my window I could just catch a glimpse of the masts and funnels of a large steamer which seemed to be lying under the lee side of the island for shelter. What she was precisely I could not see enough of her to say, nor when we met at breakfast, did the doctor know more about her.

Like many a storm that springs up very suddenly, this one began to subside as fast, and in the course of the morning I set out to have a closer look at the strange ship. Quarter of an hour's walk in that direction told me all I wanted to know about her. In fact I recognised her as no stranger at all but an old acquaintance, H.M.S. *Uruguay*, a great lump of an ex-liner once running to South American ports with a band in the saloon at nights. Now, painted grey, with the white ensign flying over her, and some hundreds of blue jackets and a formidable complement of six inch guns aboard, she was one of those auxiliary cruisers which have been doing so many odd jobs and getting through so much dirty, risky, arduous work during this war.

What had brought her under the lee of Ransay I could but guess; some engine trouble and that gale on top of it most probably, but there she was, and there were the islanders standing at each door gazing at her. I gazed too for a while and then came back to our early dinner.

J. Storer Clouston

Going out again in the afternoon, the affable Mr. Hobhouse was passing the time of day with a couple of petty officers within five minutes, and as he continued his walk he saw that, whatever was the reason, H.M.S. *Uruguay* was not going to leave immediately. The wind had now fallen to a stiff breeze, and as she lay under the shelter of the island, shore leave had evidently been given to a number of the men. First at one farm and then at another he could spy parties of blue jackets buying butter and eggs, poultry and cheeses, everything fresh from the land they could get. It was cheerful to see them again, and yet one uncomfortable thought did cross my mind as I looked at their great grey ship anchored there.

"What a sitting target for a submarine!" I said to myself. "Pray Heaven no submarine turns up here to-day!"

I had gone out to the bare northern headland and was heading home again for tea when I happened to see on the road a small knot of these blue jackets, just parting from a couple of countrymen. This pair turned towards me and in a moment I recognised my acquaintances Peter Scollay junior and Jock. Mr. Hobhouse had visited their house several times by now and was on the most friendly terms with the family.

"Good-day, Peter!" he cried as he passed them. "Have you been taking your brother to look at the ship?"

For some reason Peter stared at him in an odd way, and Jock burst into one of his loudest laughs. Peter seemed to mumble something which Mr. Hobhouse failed to catch, and then when they had passed, he could see him laughing too.

To be laughed at without knowing the reason why is always irritating, even to one of Mr. Hobhouse's exceptionally amiable temperament, and it had the effect of suddenly sharpening his critical faculties. A thing struck him that had never happened to strike him before. What was that great strapping Scollay fellow doing at home on a small croft where he was quite superfluous, when his country needed every man? And why did the lout stare and then laugh? Considering what a vigilant eye was watching him behind Mr. Hobhouse's glasses, it seemed to me unwise as well as rude.

In a moment I passed the blue jackets, who were distributing some purchases among their party before they set out for their ship, and I saw a possible excuse for Peter's amusement, though it seemed a poor one. The men were carrying a couple of baskets of eggs, two or three large cheeses, a parcel which probably contained butter, and one or two poultry. Presumably the pair had been selling them some of this assortment, and perhaps my suggestion that they had been merely sight-seeing struck them as humorous. It argued a poor sense of humour; still, there was one possibility.

Once more the amiable Mr. Hobhouse showed his friendly spirit by addressing a few kindly words to the good fellows (that was what he called them, as being the phrase most suited to his foolish appearance), and in his artless way he was able to gather that he had been correct in supposing that Peter and Jock had been amongst their purveyors. Unfortunately he had not the foresight to enquire particularly which of the articles those two had purveyed. But I wonder very much whether any possible reader of this account, given what I knew up to this point, can honestly say that he would have put that question?

Well, I got home and sat down to high tea with Dr. Rendall, and of course he began to talk of the *Uruguay's* visit. Even if nothing else had happened afterwards, such an event would have given Ransay food for several days' conversation.

"We are probably eating our last eggs and our last butter for the next week to come," he said with a laugh. "These sailors have cleared the island out, from all I can hear. They've even been to this house and got what they could, and I believe they practically cleaned out my cousin's farm."

"Really?" said Mr. Hobhouse. "Really indeed? Ha, ha! Do you know I found even the Scollays selling them things."

"Oh, I expect every one has been making hay while the sun shines," said he.

He had had one of his moody attacks so lately as the day before, but he had quite recovered his good humour by now, and in fact was in an extra jovial mood that evening. We sat up till about half-past ten, and then went up to our bedrooms.

I had reached the stage of pyjamas and was just opening my window for the night when the dreadful thing happened. Suddenly the whole island seemed to be illuminated. I turned my eyes instinctively to the place where the *Uruguay* lay, and there high into the heavens mounted a blinding pillar of flame. The wind was still blowing pretty fresh away from me and towards the ship, but even against it the roar that followed shook every window and door in the house. The pillar of flame vanished the next instant, but high in the air fire-balls seemed to linger for some minutes. And then the pillar of smoke rose up. It rose and rose, swift and gigantic, growing all the while greater and more terrible in girth, till at last when it was some hundreds of feet high it slowly stretched out at the top until it looked like some huge evil tree seen in a nightmare.

And there I stood at the window and stared. And there on the spot where H.M.S. *Uruguay* with her crew of hundreds and all her complement of officers (largely R.N.R. and R.N.V.R. men like myself) had lain, stood that gigantic pillar of smoke. Then all at once I realised that everything living in that ship and most of her inanimate self was represented now only by that foul column.

I heard the doctor's door open and his voice say: "Mr. Hobhouse! Hobhouse!"

I had presence of mind to clap my glasses hurriedly on my nose, before I rushed into the passage.

"What has happened? Is that the ship gone, do you think?" he asked in a low voice.

I noticed that he seemed a man with a good control over his feelings. I had mine, too, pretty well in hand, but to play the absurd Thomas Hobhouse at such a moment was more than I cared to do. I preferred to show a little of what I felt and get away from him on that excuse. So I stammered something, and then we looked at one another for a moment, and I hurriedly went back to my room.

J. Storer Clouston

IX

BOLTON ON THE TEACK

"Only one survivor."

The doctor looked into my room about eight o'clock next morning to give me this brief bulletin. At breakfast he told me he had been out most of the night, but there had only been that single case for him. A boat from the island had picked a solitary living seaman out of the scum of oil, blackened by it like a negro and without a stitch of clothing. Some of the dead had been found, but not in a condition to be discussed, and of course many fragments of debris. And now a number of patrol boats were on the scene, he had handed over his patient to a naval doctor, and that was all the news of the tragedy up till eight o'clock.

I knew that John Whiteclett would certainly be in one of the patrol boats, and I spent the morning in looking out for him. Thus by an apparent accident when the Commander did land about noon he very soon walked into Mr. Hobhouse. My cousin's face was grave and set, and there being no witnesses, neither of us luckily had to act.

"Well, Jack?" I said.

"Did you see it happen?" he demanded.

"I happened to be at my window."

"Tell me what you saw," said he.

I told him and he nodded at intervals.

"Just what a couple of other witnesses have told me," he said.

"Submarines?" I asked.

He shook his head.

"The odds against a torpedo sending a ship straight up like that are enormous. And one would have heard two explosions - which nobody did. Besides, the one man who was picked up has luckily been able to talk a little already. I am certain there was no torpedo attack."

"She simply blew up then?"

"That was it."

"Accident or design?"

"God knows! Perhaps no one else ever will. It may have merely been the ammunition. As you know, that has happened before now. But it's a very curious coincidence that it should have happened off Ransay, knowing what we know. I hear a lot of the men were ashore buying things. I wonder what they brought aboard with them!"

" I can tell you what one lot brought: eggs, poultry,

cheeses, and a large parcel in newspaper which I took to be butter. But that was only one party I happened to see. They were all over the island."

He thought in silence for a few moments, and then he glanced at his watch.

"Look here, old chap," he said, "I'm afraid I must be getting off again now. Walk back with me as far as it's safe and I'll tell you something that you must know. We can discuss the evidence later, when a little more has been collected. The point that concerns you is that Bolton has been sent for again."

"The devil he has! Do I retire then?"

"Not at all. You see nobody in these parts is in the Hobhouse secret, so they sent for Bolton at once to make his own kind of enquiries while we make ours. You of course go on making yours in your own way just the same. All the same I think it would be tactful to stand aside - with your eyes open of course - while Bolton is on the job."

"Tactful," I agreed, "but a little annoying."

"Well, Roger, it can't be helped, I'm afraid. I'm not the boss here and the man is on his way now as fast as he can travel. And now what about telling him who you really are? I've been thinking it over, and if you are agreeable I think I ought to."

I saw that this meant that he had decided he was going to, so I merely said:

"If you think it best, certainly tell him. Only swear him

to secrecy."

"Certainly. And I'm sure the man himself will see the point in that. But you see if I didn't tell him who you really were, he'd very likely put you down as a suspicious character and recommend your removal."

"You're quite right," I agreed.

"Besides what you know may help him, and it would be a dog in the manger kind of game to keep back anything, now that he has taken up the business."

"Right again. Well, I'll keep my nose out of the business till Bolton has had his innings."

"Good man!" said Jack. "Well, we'd better separate now. Good luck to you both!"

I trust I am not of an unduly jealous disposition, but being thus asked to take a back seat just as something really definite had happened was a strain on my philosophy. The tragedy of the *Uruguay* might not have anything to do with the secret agency in the island - though I felt in my bones it had, and Mr. Bolton might come and go and leave me possibly with a little information to help my own quest. Still, it was annoying.

At the same time, my cousin's arguments were absolutely sound and I saw perfectly that it would have been both foolish and ungenerous to play Hobhouse with the man. So I went back and picked up a novel and tried to dismiss the whole business from my mind in the meantime.

For the next twenty-four hours the island was full of gruesome stories and the wildest rumours, but for most of the time Mr. Hobhouse stayed at home and finished his novel. It was on the evening of the day after the tragedy, when the doctor and he were sitting over the smoking room fire, lighting their pipes after tea, that the bell rang. "Hallo, who's that at this hour?" said the doctor.

I heard a heavy footstep in the passage, and guessed, but the only announcement was that a gentleman wished to see Dr. Rendall. He was out of the room for a long time, nearly an hour by the clock, and when he came back his manner was serious and a little apologetic.

"I'm sorry to disturb you, Mr. Hobhouse," said he, "and I assure you there is nothing to worry about, but the fact is a detective is here and wants to have a word with you."

"A detective!" exclaimed Mr. Hobhouse nervously. "You don't say so? Dear me, what can he want me for!"

"He's a man Bolton," said the doctor, "the very man who came up about six months ago under the name of Thompson and gave himself out as a cattle dealer. By Jove, I can see now what he came for! But anyhow it's about the *Uruguay* business this time and he is interviewing everybody, and if you don't mind, he'd like a few words with you."

I went into the dining room and saw for the first time my rival. He was a big, sturdy, red-faced man, with a plain bluff manner, an ideal dealer; but his were shrewd and keen. In fact once I had looked into them I put him down as a better man than I had fancied. We exchanged a conventional word on either side, and then both of us instinctively glanced at the door.

"Better speak quietly, Mr. Merton," said he.

I nodded and said with a smile: "So you are not here as a dealer this time, Mr. Bolton?"

"No," said he, "I want to get straight to business, and there's too much humbug and waste of time if one has to talk cattle for half an hour first. Besides, after what has just happened they'd be quite sharp enough here to tumble to the game. Anyhow, the people I want to get at would be, and there's no point in humbugging the others."

"Well," I said, "you know what I'm here for, and though I'm sorry to say I haven't been able to pick up much so far, anything I have picked up is at your service."

"Much obliged, Mr. Merton," said he. "We're like a couple of terriers after the same rat, and as long as we get him that's all that matters. You've had your go and now I'm going to have a little go."

He laughed genially, but it was clear enough that when he said two terriers, he meant one terrier at a time, and I accepted the situation frankly.

"Right you are," I said. "I'll take a breather while you go in and finish him off. Only of course if you want me to lend a hand, here I am, with nothing else to do."

He seemed distinctly relieved by this declaration and grew more friendly than ever.

"Well now to come to business," he said. "I must tell you frankly in the first place, Mr. Merton, that there were some things in your story last time you were here that I didn't know just how much to believe in. The most truthful people sometimes imagine the queerest things. If you'd had my experience, Mr. Merton, you'd feel just the same about a tale like yours. But now I know you and know what's been happening here, and particularly what's happened yesterday, it's a different story. Do you mind just telling me in your own words about what you saw last time and anything you've noticed this trip?"

My opinion of Mr. Bolton's shrewdness continued to rise as I noticed his close attention to my tale and how much to the point his questions were. Every now and then he stopped me while he made a jotting in a fat little brown leather pocket book, and at the end he observed.

"Well, Mr. Merton, it's a queer case but I daresay I may be able to throw a bit of light on things before I've done."

I wondered very much, and from the look on his face I do not believe for a moment that he saw a single blink of light at that time.

"And now," said he, "coming to this explosion, I don't want to hear anything more about the flames and smoke and such like. All that is for the Navy people. It doesn't come under the head of my department, Mr. Merton; but this buying of stuff ashore and taking parcels aboard the ship, that does come under it. In fact that's what I'm up here to investigate, for it's pretty clear even to a man like me that knows nothing of ships that any one on this island couldn't swim out and hold a match to a ship o' war and blow her up that way! If it *was* done from here, it must have been by one of those parcels."

"Obviously," I agreed. "And I also agree that it's for the experts to decide whether a bomb could be slipped into a paper parcel of butter or a large cheese, or anything else they bought; and for you simply to find out exactly what was bought and who sold it."

"A paper parcel of butter and a large cheese," he repeated. "Did you happen to see any of those things being sold yourself?"

"I happened to pass some blue jackets who had just bought them."

He made me tell him exactly the circumstances of my seeing the men and my passing Peter and Jock previously; precisely in fact as I have told it in this account. He thought for a few moments in silence after I had finished and then asked me if I knew definitely of any other people who had sold anything to the sailors.

"I happen to know for certain of Dr. Rendall and his cousin Mr. Philip Rendall - or rather Mr. Philip Rendall's farmer, but from all I saw and all I heard I fancy the difficulty will be to find a house that did not sell something."

He nodded thoughtfully.

"That's exactly the difficulty," he said, and then he rose and held out his hand. "Goodnight, Mr. Merton, I'm much obliged to you and I'll promise you to make an excuse for looking you up very soon again and letting you know how I am getting on. By the way, you had better tell the doctor I was much interested in your account of how the explosion happened. That will account for my calling again."

"I must have detective instincts myself," I smiled. "I had already thought of the same lie."

In fact it came in very handy no later than Mr. Bolton's departure that night. The doctor wondered very much what the detective had to say to his patient that took him so long to tell, and his curiosity was satisfied as per arrangement.

X

WHERE THE CLUE LED

I saw nothing of Bolton next day, nor as a matter of fact did I expect to. Indeed, when he called for me on the morning after, it was a good deal sooner than I had counted on. The doctor was out, so no fable was necessary, and I took him into the smoking room and offered him an easy chair.

"Well, Mr. Bolton, any news?" I enquired.

He remained standing, and shook his head at the chair.

"I've no time to sit down," he said, "but I thought I'd just look in as I passed."

There was a note in his voice that made me look at him sharply.

"Have you discovered anything?" I asked.

He nodded his head slowly.

"Not very much, Mr. Merton, but something."

Yet there seem to be a hint of jubilation in his eye.

J. Storer Clouston

"Won't you tell the other terrier?"

His face relaxed a little and for a moment I half thought he was going to confide in me, and then he said,

"It's a little too soon to say much. But I'm on the track of something, I don't mind admitting; something pretty surprising too, if it's the right track. Possibly I may be able to tell you more to-night. Could you come out this evening with me if I needed you?"

"Rather!"

"Well," he said, moving towards the door, "any time after dark I may look in - if this leads to anything."

"Even if it doesn't, look in and put me out of suspense, like a good fellow-'tec,' Mr. Bolton."

He smiled again. Evidently he was decidedly pleased with himself this morning.

"All right, Mr. Merton. I'll do that much for you."

Just before I opened the door for him I had one last shot.

"Won't you even give me a hint, Mr. Bolton?"

He looked at me for a moment, and then said in a low voice (for we were near the door),

"There's some one in this island who hasn't lived in it all their life - not by any means. I've found that out."

He nodded significantly at me, but his lips closed tight again and I saw there was no more to be got out of him, so I wished him luck and returned to my chair to think.

Whether excitement at the prospect of actually reaching the crisis of this adventure that very night, or chagrin at seeing the problem which had eluded me solved straight off by this great drover of a fellow was my uppermost feeling, I should be afraid to say. I know both were strongly mingled and for a few minutes it never even occurred to me to question whether the man really was within sight of a solution. And then I began to wonder.

Who was this mysterious person who had not lived all "their" life on the island? He had concealed, probably deliberately, "their" sex. And was it then a fact of which I myself was unaware? Bolton said he had found it out. But it might be no news to me. I thought of several people, a woman and at least two men, who had certainly lived a considerable part of their lives out of the island. But there was no use speculating with the test so near at hand.

All the same I felt so restless that I should have gone out to walk it off there and then had it not been for the fear that I might chance to follow in Bolton's tracks and lead him to think I was doing it deliberately. At all costs I wanted him to see that I was playing the game (as I was playing it), so I waited till after our early dinner and then set off.

I well remember the day, a nasty raw specimen of March weather, not exactly raining, but trying to all the time, and altogether grey and dismal. The spring

J. Storer Clouston

ploughing was proceeding apace, and as the fields grew brown, there was less and less trace of colour left in the landscape. In fact it was a day when something evil could scarcely help happening; or at least it seems so looking back.

I walked briskly to keep the chill out, following the winding road, but so wrapt in my thoughts that I hardly noticed where I was going till I found myself passing from the metalled highway on to the rough track that led one beyond the last of the farms out to the desolate stretch of country at the nor' west end of the island. At both sides, and especially on the north, the rocks rose here till they became genuine cliffs, not very high, but rugged and broken, with little hollows dipping down through them here and there and giving scrambling access to small coves. I kept along near this northern cliff line, still thinking all the while, until with a start and a quickening of my heart I became abruptly conscious of a figure fifty yards or so ahead.

I had a sudden dim recollection; he seemed disturbingly familiar, and then in a moment I recognised Jock, though why the sight of Jock should rouse a disturbing thought was more than I could say. When I saw him he was close to one of those little dips, but whether he had been down at the shore or not, I could not say, for up to that instant I had been quite inattentive. But in any case Jock was such a chronic aimless wanderer that his appearance anywhere never surprised his acquaintances.

Evidently he recognised the harmless eccentric Mr. Hobhouse quickly enough, for he broke into a shambling trot and came towards me with an unusual air of eagerness.

"Stones!" he cried as he came up to me. "Jock knows stones!"

"Stones?" said I genially. "Dear me, Jock, this is great news. Are these the stones?" and I pointed to the rocks all about us.

"Stones here!" cried Jock pointing eagerly across towards the other side of the promontory, and catching me by the arm in a friendly way.

I had never seen the creature so excited before and for a moment could make neither head nor tail of it. And then I remembered. On my last visit to the knoll near the Scollays', Jock had been watching me, and by way of playing my part thoroughly I had affected a vast interest in certain large slabs of stone showing here and there through the grass. Looking at stones was the last thing I was keen about this afternoon, but there was simply no resisting Jock. With the air of a pleased child he led me in the way he wished me to go, only letting go my arm when he saw I really meant to inspect his stones.

"This is an unusual exhibition for Jock," I thought, but in the character of Mr. Hobhouse there was nothing for it but pretending high gratification and going where he led me.

The promontory was about a third of a mile across at this point and when we had made this journey, my intelligent guide triumphantly pointed out a few ordinary boulders at the end of it. They were large, it is true, but there their merits ended. However, I examined them with every appearance of pleasure, thanked Jock effusively and even gave him a sixpence, and at last bade him good-day and started for home.

It had been a queer little episode, and had I been in my usual clue-hunting humour I should no doubt have dissected it carefully - and then abused myself for being a fanciful fool. But this afternoon I had too much else to think of and the incident passed out of my mind in the meantime.

At tea I prepared the doctor for the possibility of my going out at night by a long-winded, babbling, and entirely fictitious account of Bolton's morning call, from which it appeared that Mr. Bolton was so interested in Mr. Hobhouse's account of how he saw the ship blow up that he would probably call in the evening to verify certain particulars and might even want Mr. Hobhouse to come with him to the house where he was lodging. And then after tea I smoked and read and waited.

Darkness was beginning to fall when we finished tea that night and the lamps were lit when we went into the smoking room. At any moment the summons might come, and yet eight o'clock struck, and nine, and ten, and I even induced the doctor to sit up till after eleven, but still there was no sign of Bolton. And then at last I said some severe things to myself about the man, and we went to bed.

Next morning was equally chilly and dismal, and after the doctor went out to visit a case, I sat over the fire resolved to stay there till Mr. Bolton came and explained himself. I stayed there all morning, but he never came, and no more did Dr. Rendall. Our dinner hour approached and passed, and at last I sat down and had my meal alone. I had just finished when I heard the front door open sharply and the doctor's step in the passage. It struck me instantly as curiously quick for him. He entered the dining room and I saw at once that something was very much the matter.

"Bolton has been murdered," he said abruptly. "His body has just been found in the sea."

XI

AN EYE-OPENER

I leapt to my feet and stared at him. "Drowned?" I gasped.

"No, he was shot first with a pistol at close quarters. I've just been examining the body."

"Where was it found?"

"Away right at the very North end."

Yesterday's episode rushed into my mind.

"At the very end?"

"Practically."

"It wasn't by any chance as much as half a mile on this side?"

He stared at me curiously and I remembered that this was certainly an odd enquiry, and also that Mr. Hobhouse was speaking very concisely.

"No," he said. "Why do you ask?"

I took refuge in an ultra-Hobhousian explanation of how I had been there myself a few days ago, and it had struck me as a very murderous looking place, and then I asked,

"Is anything more known, doctor?"

"No," he answered, and then added abruptly and with unusual energy, "This is absolutely damnable!"

He walked out of the room again as he spoke, and I was left to my thoughts. I went into the smoking room but forgot to light my pipe. With my head in my hands I bent over the fire and tried in the first place to grasp this second tragedy, and then to piece things together and see some sequence in them.

That Bolton had really been on the right scent now seemed highly probable, though as he made no concealment of his business, it was possible that an agency which had tried to murder me, defied all efforts to check it for months, and to all seeming had lately blown up a cruiser, might get rid of him simply on general principles. Still, the working hypothesis must be that he had got on to their track. And, oh, if he had only told me what he had discovered! But that secret had died with him, and now once more one must begin all over again.

Yet this time I had secured one significant-looking starting point. The coincidence of Jock's appearance out at that lonely place more or less about the time when the murder must have taken place, and his leading me away in another direction from that in which I was heading, was certainly suggestive. The creature had exhibited more appearance of intelligence than I had given him credit for, and might he not then be used by some one who knew him well and had strong influence over him, to play such a simple part as he had acted? Supposing he were with such a person and that person saw me coming and did not wish me to spy him, how easy it would be to say, "Go, Jock, and show that gentleman stones over there!"

As to whom to suspect of having such influence over him, that was easy enough. I recalled young Peter Scollay's stare and laugh when I suggested that they were going to look at the ship, and it sounded to me now a very sinister laugh.

And yet the more I thought over all this, the more objections I saw. In the first place the body was not found where I had seen Jock. True, it might have been moved if the murderer had been wily and suspicious enough to think that the simple Mr. Hobhouse was capable of connecting the harmless episode of the stones with his gruesome work, though even that seemed to imply more than was likely; but a more formidable difficulty was the evidence of educated cunning in every crime committed or attempted by that hand. For "that hand" I decided I must certainly substitute "those hands." I had always thought there was more than one in it, and now I felt surer of this than ever.

With the back of my head, as they say, I heard Dr. Rendall go into dinner and then come out again into the hall, and then I heard him, instead of coming into the smoking room, open and shut the front door. He had evidently gone out again and I was not sorry to be left alone.

A little later, in the same absent-minded way, I heard the front door bell faintly ring and I only woke out of my reverie when the smoking room door opened.

"Dr. Rendall is out, I hear," said a voice that made me jump up very hurriedly.

It was Jean Rendall, delightful to look at as ever, but with a new expression on her face. If she was not anxious, and very keenly anxious too, about something, I was much mistaken.

Unwillingly I resumed the role of Thomas Hobhouse and informed her nervously that the doctor had gone out, I knew not where.

She said nothing for a moment, but still lingered. Then she said,

"What a dreadful thing about poor Mr. Bolton!"

"Dreadful!" agreed Mr. Hobhouse. "Terrible! Dreadful! Terrible!"

"Did my cousin tell you much about it?"

"Oh, no, not much, very little. He was upset, very much upset, I could see."

"Everybody is," she said, and then added, "I should think you must be, Mr. Hobhouse."

There seemed to be an odd note in her voice set up a vague chain of disquieting emotions, but Mr. Hobhouse answered in the same tone as before:

"Oh, yes, I am distressed; dreadfully distressed."

Again she was silent, but still she lingered.

"I am going to walk home again," she said suddenly. "Would you care to walk a little way with me?"

At that moment I wanted my own company and had a certain shrinking from hers; so the voice of Mr. Hobhouse bleated something about having caught a slight chill.

"Please come a little way," she said. "I want to speak to you particularly."

There was a note of appeal in her voice which would have taken a stouter man than Thomas Hobhouse to resist. Besides, he felt exceedingly curious. Her whole manner during the interview in fact roused a very strong sensation of curiosity.

He got his hat and his coat (Mr. Hobhouse always wore a topcoat) and they crunched their way down the knobbly drive and passed out into the road, neither saying a word. And then Mr. Hobhouse got the most rousing eye-opener of his career, or of Roger Merton's either. She turned to him and said quietly,

"I hope you are taking care of your own life, Mr. Merton."

XII

THE CONFIDANT

A second or two passed before I was able to answer at all, and even then my first remark was not in the least worthy of the occasion; but it expressed precisely what was in my mind.

"How the - how on earth did you find me out?"

She smiled a little, but her manner was anxious still.

"I haven't lived all my life in Ransay," she said. "I have even been to London and to quite a good many London theatres. In fact I've seen you act before, Mr. Merton."

"What an extraordinary way to be found out!" I thought, and aloud I said,

"But my name isn't on the programme in Ransay."

"It was, when you were last here, you must remember," said she.

I looked at her for a moment, and she at me, and in that exchange of glances I decided emphatically that there was no sign of evil in those eyes. Anyhow, I stood to lose nothing if I got her confidence, and my own could

J. Storer Clouston

be withheld or not as I saw fit.

"We might as well be frank," I said. "How exactly did you come to spot me?"

Again she smiled, and each time she smiled straight at me like that, I confess frankly I grew less cautious.

"Do you remember when Captain Whiteclett came to arrest you, your bed-room door was open gust for a minute?"

I did remember now and recalled her face outside and its very expression vividly.

"I heard him call you 'Roger' and saw that you knew each other well, and then of course I knew we had been utterly wrong in thinking you a - "

She paused and I finished the sentence for her.

"A spy."

"Well, are you honestly surprised? You did do some most extraordinary things, Mr. Merton! I only began to get the least idea of what you were about some time afterwards."

"And what idea did you get then? And how did you get it?"

"It was when we began to hear of the bad name our island was getting. *Then* I guessed you must have been trying to investigate and catch the traitor - and I had gone and interfered - and even locked you up!"

"It was you, then?"

"Well, father, of course, approved, but I locked the door. And after I had found out the truth, I could have murdered myself! But why did you puzzle us so?"

Her charm and sincerity and animation almost made me tell her there and then, but I had just enough hold of myself to ask instead,

"But this doesn't explain how you came to find me out this time?"

"Well in a way it does; for I knew then that Roger Merton was your real name and then I remembered where I had heard it before, and I knew you were the same person. When you called as Mr. Hobhouse that first day I hadn't the least suspicion to begin with, and then suddenly you began to look familiar - "

"With this beard!"

"Well, your face isn't all hidden by your beard and I thought I recognised the other bits. If I hadn't known you were an actor - "

"A pretty bad one, it appears," I interposed.

"Oh, no, indeed, you were simply splendid! You still kept me puzzled and only half certain even after I had met you and Captain Whiteclett walking together and noticed you move apart when you saw me. In fact I wasn't sure till that walk along the shore. I arranged that to make quite certain."

" You arranged it! " I exclaimed. "The deuce you did,

Miss Rendall!"

She laughed defiantly.

"I was dying to make sure! So when I saw you coming towards the house, I rushed into my things and went out to meet you. I thought if I could take you the same walk as we had been before, you could hardly help doing something to give yourself away. And at last you did!"

"May I ask what my relapse was?"

"When I got you to the same place as last time and said the same thing, I noticed you jump. And then you did really rather give yourself away when I asked you if you wanted to look at the rocks, and you jumped at the chance. I know nothing about antiquities - not even as much as you do, Mr. Merton - "

"Hit me again!" I laughed.

"Oh, but it was very clever of you to pretend to be so learned!" she hastened to say. "Still, I did know that there are no antiquities below high water mark, so I knew you just wanted to inspect the place where something happened to you before."

"Where what happened?" I enquired.

"That's what I want you to tell me! Oh, if you only knew how I've died to know what happened that night!"

"How do you know anything happened?"

"I guessed," she said.

This may not sound convincing on paper, but it did as she said it. I was almost ready, in fact, to swear by Jean Rendall now.

"And so you made sure of Thomas Hobhouse!" I said. "But why then didn't you unmask him at once?"

"Oh, but it wasn't my business to! Of course I had guessed what you were doing here - "

"What?"

"Trying to rid our island of traitors of course! I had interfered with you once, but I wasn't going to do it again. In fact I tried to reassure you by talking of my walk with Mr. Merton."

"Miss Rendall," I said, "I am a child at this game. You did reassure me. I have been as clay in your hands. But tell me one thing more. Why on earth did you come out with me on that first walk - armed with that horse pistol?"

"Oh, you saw it then!" she exclaimed.

"I almost smelt the slow match! But why did you do it?"

"Well, you know what I thought you were then, and there was no one else to go with you."

"Then you actually went out with a spy at night to keep an eye on him - and shoot him if he spied?"

"I should probably have missed!" she laughed.

I was quite ready to swear by Jean Rendall now. Talk of pluck! I never heard of a more fearless performance!

"Please understand, Mr. Merton," she went on earnestly, "that I should never have dreamt of letting you know that I had recognised you - I haven't even told father, I assure you! - only when I heard of this dreadful death of Mr. Bolton - "

She paused and glanced at me, half apologetically, half beseechingly, it seemed.

"Well?" I said.

"Well, I realised the danger you were in supposing anybody else guessed. And I thought I'd come and speak to you. I'm afraid I sometimes act on impulse."

"So do I," I confessed. "In fact I'm going to act on impulse now. Do you care to hear some bits of the story you don't know?"

Her eyes absolutely danced.

"Oh, I'd love to! I've been longing - dying to know the rest of it! I've guessed and guessed, but I haven't been able to make any sense out of things!"

I remembered my uncle's injunctions distinctly. I also remembered my cousin's cautions and my own good resolutions. A woman, of all things, I was to beware of; but I knew I was perfectly safe to throw overboard the whole collection of cautions: and already I had a strong suspicion I should be far from a loser by it. Miss

Rendall seemed, in fact, to have distinctly more natural capacity for detective work than I had, judging by her performances so far.

So I plunged straight into the tale of my first landing on Ransay and my adventure with the oilskinned man on the shore, and may I always have as attentive an audience when I tell a story.

"So there is actually a German who dares to live on Ransay!" she exclaimed, her cheeks flushing a little.

"A man whom I certainly took to be a German - a man who talks German fluently."

She fell very thoughtful and presently repeated,

"Middle-sized - with a beard - and dark eyes?"

"Yes," I said confidently; for somehow or other I began to feel singularly sure of these features.

"Of course I know who you suspect," she said, looking up suddenly. "And you had him removed from the island afterwards."

"You mean O'Brien? Yes, I did suspect him - though, mind you, I had nothing to go on. Do you know if he talked German?"

"He once told me he did, but I never heard him, and I didn't believe him."

"Why not?"

" One couldn't believe half he said, and I don't think he

intended one to. He was very Irish. But I don't believe he was the man."

"Why not?" I asked again.

"Oh, just because I don't. And what happened next?"

I told her of my night at the Scollays' and my plan for trapping the spies. My self-respect as a criminal catcher was distinctly soothed to hear her hearty approval of this scheme.

"It was awfully ingenious," she said decidedly. "I can't imagine a better plan, and you did it so well that you took us all in completely. I suppose you felt you had to count us among the suspicious characters, but what a pity you hadn't confided in father or me as it happened! We would have done everything we could to help you. I'd have loved to spread dreadful rumours about you!"

"I'm sure you would," I said, "but as things turned out, and in the light of what has happened since, I believe you saved my life by arresting me."

She turned on me and asked breathlessly.

"Did they guess who you really were? Did they try to do anything to you?"

"Merely murder me, as they murdered poor Bolton. The first attempt was made that night on the shore."

I saw her lips parting as I neared the end of telling her that story, and the instant I finished she cried,

"Of course you thought it was father!"

I did my best to shuffle out, but she was a hopeless person to try to deceive.

"It was quite natural you should," she said, "but I can tell you something now that throws some light on things. Next morning I heard that a man had been calling for you after dinner and was told that you had gone out with me. And the funny thing was that the maid didn't know him by sight, or know his voice. He kept his face rather hidden, she said, and talked in a low voice. Of course it simply increased our suspicions of you. But that was how they knew where you were! And that was the man who tried to kill you."

"And who'd have done it for certain if he had found me at home that night," I added.

I must frankly confess that this little incident made me feel uncomfortable. The audacity of the steps my enemies took, their remorseless thoroughness, the extraordinary completeness with which they covered their tracks, their appearances from nowhere and disappearances into space, were particularly nasty to contemplate with Bolton's fate so fresh in my mind.

"They are pretty thorough," I said.

She seemed to divine the thoughts behind this remark.

"But they haven't suspected you yet," she said reassuringly, "and they mustn't! And now, tell me some more, Mr. Merton."

So I went on telling her more: - about the man with spectacles, the shooting episode, every single thing in fact I could remember. As we neared the house we walked more and more slowly, but my tale was barely finished when we got there.

"You'll come in, won't you?" she said. "I know father is out, so we can go on talking."

She saw me hesitate and her colour faintly rose.

"You do trust me now, surely!" she said.

"All the way, Miss Rendall. But these devils may be on to my track at any moment, and if they suspect you are in my confidence - "

"What nonsense!" she cried, "if there's any risk I *want* to share it. For the credit of our island these people have got to be hunted down, and I'd like them to know I'm hunting them! Besides, there's rather a nice cake for tea; you must come in."

And in we went.

XIII

JEAN'S GUESSES

"Come into father's room and then you can smoke," said Jean.

It was the same pleasant, well-remembered room into which she had shown me that day when I first made her acquaintance, and as I followed her in now it struck me forcibly that I had taken the wrong turning that August morning. If I had taken these people into my confidence then, I should at least have started on the right road. Better than ever I realised what tricks my instincts play me. Or perhaps it may be my efforts to regulate them by the light of what I am pleased to call my reason that produce such unhappy results.

"I am wondering how they found you out," she began. "It seems so mysterious that they should have suddenly started to try and murder you like that. They must have felt quite positive - and what made them feel positive?"

"Did you or your father say anything to anybody about my voice; that I didn't seem to have so much accent as I had at first, or anything of that kind?"

"Not a word," she said positively. "Father is the most uncommunicative of people, and I have inherited some

J. Storer Clouston

of his closeness."

"Your servants?" I suggested.

"They are Ransay girls, and one foreign accent is the same as another to them," she laughed.

"Then it must have been finding the parachute. I always thought that gave me away."

"But it wasn't found till Monday morning, after we had been for that walk."

"It might have been found by these people sooner."

"It might," she admitted without much conviction. "But still - who did you see or speak to apart from us and Dr. Rendall and Mr. O'Brien?"

"The Scollays," I said, "and several farmers I happened to meet; but always with a most suspicious accent. Oh, and there was one incident I forgot to mention. On the Sunday afternoon I was doing a little fancy shooting with my revolver down on the beach when Jock turned up. You know Jock the idiot?"

"Well," she said, but her attention had evidently been caught by my first words. "You were doing fancy shooting," she repeated. "Are you a very good shot?'

"Quite useful," I admitted with becoming modesty. "That afternoon I was rather above myself."

"Then," she cried, "you were seen, and that's why the man stopped firing at you as soon as you aimed at him! He knew he would be hit if he went on!"

I opened my eyes a little and smiled.

"That is a flattering solution," I said, "but if I may venture to say so, it seems rather a bold inference."

"I'm certain it's right," she said confidently. "Did you speak to Jock?"

"Yes, I had a little talk with him; that's to say of course I did all the talking."

"In your natural voice?"

"Latterly I did," I admitted.

"Were you far from the wall above the beach."

"Not very."

"And I suppose there were lots of rocks about?"

"The usual supply."

"Then some one was behind either the wall or the rocks and you were overheard! That's how you were found out!"

"Miss Rendall," I said, "you arrive at solutions by such brilliant short cuts that I feel like an old cart horse stumbling along out of sight behind you. My models hitherto have been the classical detectives - "

"Tuts!" she laughed, "they were only men!"

"Yes," I agreed, "we are not much of a sex. And now, guess again please, it's a very simple conundrum this time - for you. Who was the man behind the wall - or the rocks?"

She looked the least trifle hurt.

"I am really trying to help," she said,

"I know it!" I assured her. "And don't think I am laughing at you. This jumping to conclusions is probably the right way of reaching them. Anyhow my way has failed, and I am only too keen to try yours."

But I could see that I had a sensitive as well as a clever ally, and her ardour was evidently a little damped. I tried my best to rekindle it.

"I haven't told you yet," I said, "about Mr. Hobhouse's attempts at detection. He discovered one little fact. The old man with the tinted spectacles was seen by a small child running towards the beach after he had interviewed me."

I could see her pricking up her ears again, but she said little this time, and I went on to tell her of Bolton's two talks with me. When I came to his discovery her ardour was fairly aflame again, yet she still seemed to be holding herself in a little.

"Some one who hasn't lived all 'their' life in the place," she repeated. "Yes, it sounds as if he meant a woman."

"Oh, I didn't say that," I interposed.

"You thought it," she retorted, "and in that case I suppose it was me."

"But surely he must have known that before!"

"One would think so," she said thoughtfully, "but he didn't look a very intelligent man - poor fellow! Still, it would be a stupid kind of discovery to make a fuss about."

"There's just one thing more to tell you," I said; and I told her of the curious episode by the cliffs on the day Bolton was murdered, and mentioned my own conclusions, such as they were, and my difficulties in fitting them into the evidence.

There was no doubt about her keenness now, yet I noticed that there were no bold inferences this time. Nor did she even ask me many questions. But I saw her grow very thoughtful.

"Well," I said, "have you any ideas - any suspicions?"

She gave no answer for a few moments, and then she said.

"I am not going to jump to conclusions again, Mr. Merton. There is no use trying to act on wild ideas till we have found a little more out. You might just be running risks for no purpose, and you are in quite enough danger as it is."

"Hobhouse will look after me," I assured her.

She glanced at me with a look in her eyes that gave me a little thrill, and then I saw a slight shiver run over her.

" You are too brave to realise what danger you are in!

Remember Bolton!"

"Believe me, Miss Rendall, I am just as careful of my skin as other people, but there is absolutely no danger so long as they don't spot me."

"But how long will that be? And you are taking no precautions at all!"

"But I am! I assure you I am. I have a code wire arranged with my cousin and when he gets the message 'Request permission to be visited by my own doctor,' he will be in Ransay as fast as he can steam."

She gave a little laugh, but looked anxious still.

"What a delicious message! Well, that's better than nothing. But you don't imagine they will give you warning, do you?"

"You will," I said confidently. "When you guess there's danger I'll wire. And now, I hope you have some idea in your head besides this notion of my danger. Be honest! what's in your mind?"

But I now perceived I had also an obstinate ally.

"I have told you," she persisted, "we must find out a little more before doing anything rash. And I promise not to keep anything back, and to tell you at once if I find out anything worth knowing. Oh, if you only knew how I want you to catch those people! As if I could possibly do anything again to interfere with you!"

What I should have liked to do was to take her hands

and say something very friendly. What I did do was to thank her and assure her I trusted her, in words that I think she knew were sincere; and arrange to see her accidentally next day. And then I set off for my sanatorium with thoughts that were not in the least of the detective type.

It was Jean Rendall's eyes, voice, smile and face - herself from her hair to her ankles - that filled my mind as I hummed my way home. Unlike the suspicious stranger, Thomas Sylvester Hobhouse had not been given to singing, whistling, or humming as he walked, but he broke loose now. I had instinctively dreaded a too close acquaintance with that girl while the case was doubtful. I felt in my bones she would be dangerous. Now I was enraptured to discover she was fatal.

XIV

THE POCKET BOOK

Out of the doctor's smoking-room window you saw nothing but a field or two of bleached wintry grass, with a glimpse of grey sea beyond and that iniquitous pebble drive close at hand. That at least was all I could see on the blighting March morning after my tea with Jean Rendall. The chilly damp weather had given place to chillier hard weather. With the temperature below freezing and thin showers of dry snow driving up every now and then before a biting nor'east wind, there was little temptation to go abroad without excuse. My excuse was due in an hour's time when Miss Rendall and Mr. Hobhouse proposed to encounter one another accidentally on the road, and meantime I was turning away from the window towards the fire when I heard the gravel crunch.

On general principles I turned back and looked out, to see a certain small farmer approaching the front door. I knew the man slightly and was not in the least interested in him. Presumably, I thought, it was a call for the doctor; and then my attention was sharply caught. He was carrying in his hand a fat little brown leather pocket book and in an instant I had remembered where I had seen exactly such a pocket book before.

A minute or two later it so chanced that as the maid was speaking to the man at the door, the amiable Mr. Hobhouse came out into the hall, and in his friendly way approached to see what the matter was; and very interested indeed he became when he heard. The pocket book, said the farmer, bore the name of James Bolton inside, and the maid was shuddering over a dull stain on the cover when Mr. Hobhouse appeared. The man went on to explain that he and a friend had been visiting the scene of the tragedy early that morning and had discovered the pocket book among the rocks close to where the body had been found. The local police had been in the island and visited the spot yesterday afternoon, he said, and he had meant to give his find to them, but now he heard that they had left again. They were coming back, and London police with them, people said, but meanwhile he thought the pocket book should be deposited either with the doctor or the laird (being Justices of the Peace), and he had called at the doctor's first. Now, the doctor being out, he meant to take it to Mr. Rendall's.

Hardly necessary to say, Mr. Hobhouse instantly took upon himself the responsibility of seeing that the doctor got the pocket book the moment he returned, and the farmer, glad enough to save himself a longer walk, handed it over. And then Mr. Hobhouse put a few very natural questions.

"Was the pocket book wet when it was found?"

"No wetter than she is now," said the man.

"Then it must have fallen out of poor Bolton's pocket before his body was thrown into the sea! Dreadful! Dreadful!" exclaimed the distressed gentleman. "And was it quite conspicuous - easily seen on the rocks?"

"We saw it a' right," said the man.

"And yet the police never noticed it? Dear me, dear me! Well, well, I'll give it to the doctor. Good morning, my good fellow, and many thanks; good morning!"

Over the smoking room fire I examined this discovery very thoughtfully. That it should have lain on the rocks all the time, and nobody, not even the police, noticed it till now, seemed strange. Still, when one came to think of it, the brown colour was very like the seaweed, and among that jumble of boulders such a thing might readily have happened. But certainly it had fallen out before the body was thrown into the sea, as its condition proved.

I glanced through the entries till I came to the very last the poor man had made; and then I sat up and opened my eyes very wide indeed. Plainly and distinctly these mems. were jotted:

"Proof positive O'B. or confederate.

"To be discovered whether O'B. himself - or the other?

"Possibilities - Thomsons - No Scotts - No Scollays - No."

The Thomsons and Scotts I knew to be tenants of seaboard farms like the Scollays, and after the Scollays came three other names, each with "No" written after them. A pencil mark also scored across all the six names.

So here was Bolton's secret. Either O'Brien was actually in the island himself, or he had a "confederate" here, and since that entry was made, one of the two had crowned his series of crimes by murdering the man who was on his track. And who was this confederate? Or alternatively, where was O'Brien himself lurking? Obviously the six names were people definitely acquitted, in Bolton's estimation anyhow; for the "No" and the line through their names could only mean that.

In this list certain names were not included - I had got so far when I happened to glance at the clock and started to my feet. My appointment with Jean was already overdue.

No sign of her when I reached the road, so I set off to walk slowly towards her house, thinking, thinking, thinking. Of course the man most of all to be suspected was her own cousin. And if he were in it, I knew that any person of common sense would warn me to beware of confiding in his only relatives in the island. But I felt sure I knew better than any person of mere common sense. Still, I could scarcely ask her to abet me in convicting the doctor. Then I must not show her the note book. And that meant a breach in our confidence at the very start.

I had walked on till I was approaching her house, and still there was no sign of her ahead, nor was there any conclusion in my mind. And then I chanced to look round and saw her hastening after me, about a couple of hundred yards away. I wheeled round and on the instant leapt to one of my typical haphazard decisions. I would simply show her the pocket book and see how she took it.

J. Storer Clouston

She had evidently been running and met me half cross and half laughing and divinely flushed after her stern chase.

"I've been chasing you for miles!" she cried. "Why ever didn't you look round?"

"But I thought you were coming straight from home!"

"I never said so, and I wasn't! I've been somewhere else first."

There seemed to be a hint of something significant in these last words, but I was so eager to come to the point that I never paused to question her.

"I am dreadfully sorry," I said, "but I was thinking so hard I never thought of looking round. I have got some news for you."

Her eyes sparkled.

"What is it?" she cried.

"Bolton's pocket book has been found among the rocks, and this was his last entry before he was killed."

I handed her the book open at the place and watched her face as she read. And one thing her expression revealed beyond any possibility of doubt. She was utterly and completely taken aback, and for some moments simply stared at the jottings in dead silence. Then I saw a sudden gleam in her eye, and a moment later she turned to me and cried,

"This wasn't written by Bolton!"

It was my turn to stare.

"Not written by Bolton!" I exclaimed. "Let me look at it again."

Standing there in the middle of the windy road, we quite forgot the temperature, and a passing snow shower even whipped us unnoticed.

"Look!" she said. "The writing is thicker and blacker and a little bigger than the other entries."

"It was evidently written with a different pencil, or with a blunt pointed pencil. A man writing with a short blunt stump naturally writes a little bigger and blacker. But look at the *t*s and the *r*s, and the capital *P;* in fact, look at all the letters. They are exactly the same type."

"Of course any one trying to copy another man's hand would make his letters the same," she retorted, "but the character isn't the same. Can't you see?"

"There is a slight difference," I admitted, "but I really can't honestly say I see any sufficient ground for putting this down as a fake. Besides, what do you suppose it is - a practical joke?"

"No, of course not. It was written by the real murderer to put people off the scent."

I tried not to smile, but I am afraid I did.

"Another brilliant guess!" I said, and then hastened to add, "But a most ingenious one and quite possibly - very probably, in fact, you are right."

But she saw through my compliments, and I felt rather than observed an instant change in her.

"Oh, you may be right," she said, and handed me back the pocket book.

"Or wrong," I replied, "but I mean to try and discover which."

Instead of asking me what I meant to do, as I feared and expected, she walked by my side very thoughtfully and in silence. I gave her a moment or two to put the question which never came, and then changed the subject.

"And have you discovered anything?" I asked.

"Not discovered - only guessed," she answered with a smile in her eyes, half defiant, half mischievous.

"And what have you guessed?"

"Oh, I won't trouble you with more guesses. I must find something out first - something really convincing, like that note book."

I was a little piqued, but I merely laughed and said,

"Well, we'll see!"

By this time we were quite near the house.

"Won't you come in and have lunch with us?" she asked.

The temptation was strong, but the scent seemed too

warm to lose, and I said I must be back for lunch at home. We stopped, and as she looked at me I noticed in her eyes what first seemed to be doubt and anxiety and a moment later to become resolution.

"Mr. Merton," she said; her voice rather low, "which ever of us is right, I think we must be getting near rather a critical point. Don't you think you had better send off that wire to Captain Whiteclett?"

I shook my head.

"Not quite yet," I said. "You see it's a serious matter dragging my cousin out here unless one is quite certain he will be needed."

"But then he may not be in time!"

"I must risk that. But you may rest assured I'll wire the very instant I know it won't be bringing him out on a wild goose chase."

For an instant she was silent again, and then she suddenly said,

"I'm sure that writing was forged!"

It seemed to me that I read in her exclamation a kind of whipping up of her unbelief, as though she needed to reassure herself.

"A pair of gloves on it?" I suggested.

I quite confess that it was not one of my most tactful suggestions. She froze up again at once. Not that there was anything unkind in her eye as we said good-bye, only it was clear that in the meantime we were each going our own way.

I set out at my best pace back for I was hot for instant action, and Jean's doubts, though I dismissed them as quite unjustified by anything in the writing, nevertheless made me anxious to settle the question at once. The end might be very near indeed, I told myself, as I strode out with the last remains of my limp quite vanished. But what prompted those doubts; a genuine disbelief in the authenticity of the handwriting, or a perception of the logical consequences and a very natural shrinking from them? I wondered very much. The fact that she had refrained from asking a single question as to what I meant to do, suggested the second solution. And yet it was curiously unlike Jean Rendall's fearless spirit.

XV

PART OF THE TRUTH

I never remember feeling more intensely chagrined than when I reached our bleak house twenty minutes late for our early dinner to find the doctor had eaten a hurried meal quarter of an hour before the usual hour and rushed out to attend an urgent case.

I asked at once whether he had been told of the pocket book. Yes, it appeared he had. He had seemed very interested, but had immediately ordered his dinner hour to be advanced and then hurried away without putting further questions.

Was his haste a consequence of what he was told, or merely a coincidence? Well, I was resolved to leave that point in doubt no later than his return. I hardly debated at all the question of what to do. The baffling business of groping in the dark, and daily scheming to discover a window, without giving myself away, had gone on long enough. I had found a head at last and I meant to hit it. It might turn out to be the wrong head; still, I felt convinced I could scarcely fail to discover something fresh.

But though I proposed to take a bold course and make a short cut to the heart of this infernal mystery, I realised perfectly that if the cut actually led me there, it would prove an exceedingly dangerous by-way. It was such a gamble that I shrank from summoning my cousin until it had come off, but I wrote out the code telegram we had arranged and put it in my pocket ready for emergencies. Of the doctor's two servants the younger anyhow was absolutely trustworthy I was convinced, and I meant to send her with the wire to the post office while I kept guard over the prisoner. And then, to ensure there being a prisoner, I saw that all the chambers of my revolver were loaded and put it in my coat pocket ready to my hand.

The afternoon dragged on, the wind still blustering round the house and the hail now and then rattling on the windows; but no Dr. Rendall appeared. Tea time arrived and still no sign of him. I gave him half an hour's grace and then had my own tea and returned to the smoking-room. The evening by this time had fallen and the curtains were drawn and the lamps lit.

And then at last I heard him enter the front door. I jumped up and, with a dramatic instinct for taking the centre of the stage, placed myself before the fire, but I heard him run upstairs and it was some minutes before the sound of his descending steps reached me. The moment the door opened I was conscious that one of those peculiar changes I had so often noticed had taken place in the man. He smiled at me, but with a curiously furtive eye, and then he shut the door and came forward.

"You have had tea, I hope," said he.

I wasted no time in preliminaries. Keeping my right hand closed over the revolver in my pocket I held out the pocket book with my left.

"Dr. Rendall," I said, "you have heard that Bolton's pocket book has been found. Here it is. Kindly look at that entry."

The man started perceptibly and stared at me. Speaking in that tone and without my eye glasses I must have made an astonishing contrast to the Thomas Hobhouse he had last seen that morning at breakfast.

"Read that," I commanded.

He took the pocket book and I watched him closely. I saw his eyebrows rise as he read.

"What's all this about?" he asked.

"It is Bolton's last entry in his note book before he was murdered, and it means that O'Brien is either still in this island, or that a confederate of his is playing traitor in his place, and that one of the two has just committed murder. It is quite impossible that you don't know something of this!"

His blue eyes now had considerably more anger than guilt in them. In fact I was bound to admit that he looked a fine upstanding man, with his grey moustache, high colour, and an air of unmistakable indignation in his face.

"Who the devil are you?" he demanded.

"I may tell you that I am *not* Thomas Sylvester Hobhouse, and that I have never taken liquor enough in my life to hurt myself. I am here to investigate certain things that have been going on in this island, and I'll put one question to you straight, Dr. Rendall. You remember being visited by a certain man Merton last August, When you heard him approaching your house why did you pull down your blind?"

That shot went straight home. All the indignation vanished and I saw on the instant I had him at my mercy.

"What - what - has that to do with it?" he stammered.

"Don't trouble to try and hedge. As a matter of fact I am Merton and I saw the blind go down myself. Since then we have always been on your tracks, Dr. Rendall."

"I swear that that had nothing to do with treason!"

"You are accused of treason, your relations to O'Brien were very peculiar, and if you can't explain that blind and this entry and a number of other things, you will be in an extremely nasty position."

The doctor made no further effort to stand up to me. He sank into a chair while I stood over him, and I knew I was going to hear the truth at last. And yet this sudden collapse, and indeed his whole attitude, were so unexpected that I felt more puzzled than triumphant.

"Mr. Merton," he said, "for God's sake don't give me away and I'll tell you the whole truth. My cousin Philip can confirm it - or at least part of it. I came up here because - well, I'd married the wrong woman and gone off the rails a bit and Philip settled me here to keep me straight. I had debts too - I have them still, I may tell you frankly. That's why I took in O'Brien. I wasn't supposed to keep any liquor in the house - that was one of the conditions. But damn it, I wasn't born to be a teetotaler, and that's the plain truth, Mr. Merton. That devil O'Brien found me out and started to black-mail me - "

"Blackmail?" I asked.

"In his own way. He made me give him liquor - and there we were the pair of us! That's why I pulled down the blind. The decanter and glasses were all out on this table here! And that's why O'Brien was afraid you might be sent by his relations. That was the one thing he was afraid of, - that he might be found out and taken away."

I bent over him and sniffed.

"You have had a dram now!" I exclaimed.

"And it's not the first since you've been here either. You see I'm perfectly frank with you, Mr. Merton. If you like to give me away to Philip - well be d - d, you can if you like. But you'll surely not? I've told you what I've told to no one else."

There rushed into my mind confirmation enough of part at least of the poor devil's story. His curious moods, his manner as he entered the room this evening, O'Brien's impish allusions to liquor when I first visited the house, all fell into their places now. Yet utterly as this had exploded my hopes, I think I was more glad than sorry to see the doctor come out of the ordeal with only this kind of stain on his character. He was a likeable man , we had been capital friends - and he was Jean's cousin.

"I promise you, doctor," I said, "that I shall repeat no word of this story - except of course in confidence to those who are on the track of this business in Ransay. Only in return you must tell me absolutely frankly if you have seen any grounds for suspecting O'Brien of anything treasonable - anything whatever."

The doctor shook his head emphatically.

"The only plotting the man was capable of was to get liquor. Otherwise he was just a gas bag. I've seen him too often in a state when he'd have given everything away, if there had been anything to give."

And then I remembered the pocket book.

"But this entry!" I cried. "How do you explain that?"

The doctor looked at it again and his bewilderment was obviously sincere.

"I'm frankly d - d if I can make head or tail of it," he said. "Bolton must have got on the wrong scent; that's the only thing I can imagine."

And then, like a sharp smack in the face, Jean's reading of that entry came back to me. Could she have guessed right after all? It looked uncommonly like it.

"And yet," I said to myself, "it's a great thing to have tested the other hypothesis."

In fact, if one is not built to be easily dispirited, well, it is not easy to dispirit one. I looked at the doctor, and something in my expression seemed to make him smile. When he smiled he looked so pleasant that my conscience smote me. I told myself he certainly deserved some reparation for the ordeal I had put him through.

"Doctor," I said, "I am devilish thirsty myself after this bout. Let's each have a whisky and soda!"

It may or may not have been the wisest suggestion to make. I am not an expert in these matters. But anyhow if he enjoyed his drink as much as I enjoyed mine, it was at least a happy idea.

We had lit our pipes with our glasses at our sides, and I was in the midst of giving the doctor some further reparation in the shape of the true tale of my adventures, when I saw him suddenly start and glance guiltily at his tumbler.

"Is that some one in the hall?" he exclaimed.

"Probably the servants," I suggested.

The next instant the door opened and, without any announcement, in walked my uncle Sir Francis Merton followed by my cousin Commander John Whiteclett.

XVI

TRACKED DOWN

"I trust we are not interrupting you, Roger," said my uncle.

His voice was caustic and his eye severe, and as the costume he had selected for this thunderbolt entrance was apparently designed to suggest a combination of North Sea pilot and pirate King (including a fur cap with ear flaps tied under his venerable chin) one might have fired a twelve inch gun into the room and produced much less impression.

"Not a bit," I said, bounding to my feet, "but - er - wouldn't you like to untie your bonnet, Uncle Francis?"

He frowned at me heavily but I was thankful to notice that his eye did twinkle for an instant.

"What is the meaning of this?" he demanded.

"That is just the question, sir, I was going to put."

My cousin interposed.

" Uncle Francis arrived this morning to see how things

were getting on and when I got your wire I brought him out with me. What has happened?"

"Got my wire!" I exclaimed. "Surely - I'm certain I never sent it off!"

I put my hand in my pocket, and there it was right enough.

"My dear Jack, here it is. It never was sent."

His hand dived into his own pocket and then held out a crumpled telegram. I took it and read this message.

"Request permission to be visited by my own doctor. Hobhouse."

"Do you mean to say you never sent that off yourself?" exclaimed Sir Francis.

"Never!"

"Then who the - !" My uncle's expression completed the sentence.

Jack Whiteclett was looking uncommonly grave.

"This is a somewhat serious matter, Roger," he said quietly. "Didn't you write this either?"

He handed me a half sheet of paper on which was written in pencil these words.

"GO TO DOCTOR'S. IF NO FURTHER MESSAGE THERE GO ON TO SCOLLAYS' *IMMEDIATELY*."

J. Storer Clouston

It was printed in capital letters so as to give no clue to the handwriting.

"When did you get that?" I cried.

"It was handed to me as we landed. The messenger went off again at once, but I assumed of course it was from you."

"Roger!" thundered my uncle. "Who have you taken into your confidence?"

His eye turned manacingly on the doctor and I hastened to intervene.

"Dr. Rendall - Sir Francis Merton," I introduced. "But it certainly wasn't Dr. Rendall who sent these messages. He has only just learned the facts."

My uncle bowed very stiffly to the doctor and turned on me again.

"And how many more people have 'learned the facts' - the facts, I may remind you, which it was so vital they should *not* learn?"

I bared my metaphorical breast, and with as close an imitation of a clear-conscienced young man revealing the harmless necessary truth as I could achieve without rehearsal, I told him,

"I have only informed one person, and she is thoroughly trustworthy."

"She!" said my uncle, not very loudly but extremely unpleasantly.

"She is Miss Rendall," I added.

My revelations to the doctor not having reached this stage when we were interrupted, I think I can honestly say that no utterance of mine ever produced a more telling effect on these men simultaneously.

"Jean!" exclaimed the doctor.

"Oh, is that her name?" said my uncle as soon as he could trust himself to speak.

My cousin alone came straight to the point.

"Then she has sent me this wire and this message?"

"She must have," I agreed.

"In that case we had better push on for the Scollays at once and see what she means."

"You don't think it's a trap?" asked my uncle.

Jack Whiteclett smiled slightly. The idea of the Navy pausing to weigh the risk appeared to amuse him.

"We must take our chance," he said briefly. "We've both got our shooting irons."

"And so have I," I added, "and certainly *I* am going to the Scollays. You can trust Miss Rendall!"

"You can that!" said the doctor heartily. "And if you don't mind I'll come with you."

I saw doubt in my uncle's eye and put in quickly.

J. Storer Clouston

"Certainly, doctor! We may all be needed. Come on!"

It was quite dark, and mortal cold; the road was frozen hard and the nor'east wind swept over it without a break from wall or hedge-row. We all four trotted for a little to get up our circulation and then settled down to a fast five-mile-an-hour walk. About half the distance had been covered when I first heard a little sound ahead.

"What's that!" I exclaimed, and we stood still and listened.

"Somebody running!" said my cousin.

"Towards us?" asked Sir Francis.

"Yes."

Plainer and plainer sounded the pattering steps on the frozen road, and as they drew nearer I thought I could tell that they were light steps - a woman's or a boy's, they seemed.

"Let's drop into the ditch and see who it is," whispered Jack.

We broke, two of us to either side of the road, and I found myself with my uncle stooping in one ditch, with Jack and the doctor across the road in the other. Thus bent down, one could see objects against the sky more distinctly and in a moment I spied the runner dimly, pattering down the middle of the road straight for us. And then, in a few seconds, this runner gradually took shape and my eyes at last could see the swing of a skirt and thought they could even recognise the slim figure. I jumped up.

"Wait!" muttered my uncle.

"It's all right! We mustn't frighten her," I said.

I came out into the middle of the road and saw the other three rising at the sides. The runner was barely twenty yards away by now and I heard her gasp as she stopped abruptly.

"Miss Rendall?" I said.

The next moment she had rushed up to me, her eyes sparkling, her voice coming in pants.

"Mr. Merton!" she panted and then her eyes fell on the others. "They've come then - I'm so glad! - forgive me for wiring - but - look!"

She handed me something small and long-shaped. It was a spectacle case.

"Take them out!" she said.

We were all four gathered round her now and I heard my uncle say,

"Where's that torch of yours, Jack?"

Then the flash of my cousin's electric torch fell on the spectacles and my heart leapt.

"The tinted spectacles!" I cried.

" Where did you find them?" demanded my uncle and

cousin simultaneously, and I could tell from their voices that all doubts had vanished, and that, like me, they were burning now only with the excitement of the chase.

"At the Scollays'!" she said, still panting. "But there's no time to lose - you'll see everything if we only hurry - he may be back if we don't!"

Sir Francis (of course) pocketed the spectacle case, and the whole five of us set out at the double, Jean trotting in front between Jack and me, and Sir Francis and the doctor clattering behind. My cousin and I each tried a question, but we saw that Jean's breath would be better saved for whatever was ahead, and so our voices fell silent and presently as we left the high road our feet fell almost silent too. We only dropped to a walk when the farm buildings loomed up close ahead, and then for a moment Jean stopped us and listened intently.

"They are all in the house still," she whispered. "I think we are in time!"

She led us, walking in single file and on our toes, into the midst of the huddle of low houses until we came to one open, pitch-dark door. And then she flashed a little torch and we followed her into a building which I remembered distinctly. One end was the barn where I slept that memorable first night in Ransay. The other was filled with a litter of odds and ends - coils of rope, fishing nets, a barrel or two, spades, a pick-axe, and I cannot remember what else. With feverish energy she pushed and pulled these things aside, my cousin's torch lighting up the jumble, until a large rough wooden box became visible, standing in the very corner against the wall. I could see at a glance that it had been locked and the lock forced.

"I broke it open!" she whispered. "So there was no time to lose or he'd have known!"

We raised the heavy lid and the very first thing my eyes fell on was a white false beard. Jean picked it up and I could hear her voice shaking with excitement.

"There's the rest of the disguise!" she said.

And there was the old coat, and a nasty looking scythe blade, and a number of other things of which the powers that be have an inventory now, but which they would scarcely thank me for mentioning here. I may say, however, that they made a very thorough outfit for the job the owner of them had been engaged on. Among them was one very curious looking find: the two halves of a large cheese hollowed out, and one-half broken across. Jack Whiteclett pointed to this with a grim look.

"An unsuccessful experiment," he whispered. "He must have made a better one for the *Uruguay*"

"Do you mean," gasped Jean, "that this was for a bomb?"

"Looks like it," he answered.

"Hush!" I whispered.

The torch went out on the instant and in absolute inky darkness we held our breath and listened. Somebody was quietly approaching the barn. The steps were not exactly stealthy, but guarded and wary, though quite assured, as if the man were only exercising a general precaution.

"Keep your faces hidden as much as you can!" whispered Whiteclett.

There was enough light in the open door to silhouette a figure as it entered, and a moment later I saw for an instant quite distinctly the outline of that oilskinned man once more. And then for perhaps three long seconds he was lost in the gloom within and we only knew of his approach by the sound of his footsteps. Abruptly they stopped. He was little more than a couple of paces from us now and I thought I heard him move back a step. Probably he had seen the white of some one's face.

There was a little click and Whiteclett's torch flashed full on him. In that instant I saw his hand rise, and with my head down I charged him. The report of his pistol rang through the barn and almost simultaneously down he came, and I had a firm grip of those oilskins at last.

How the man fought! Not till I was sitting on his legs and Jack and the doctor each had an arm pinned to the floor did he cease to struggle, and even then he did not cease to swear. Sir Francis standing up over him, with the torch in his own hand, now turned the light on to his face. When I saw what it revealed I nearly let go our prisoner's legs through sheer bewilderment. For there in the torch's bright circle lay the poor idiot Jock, cursing us in fluent German.

XVII

THE REST OF THE TRUTH

"Does any one know him?" demanded my uncle.

"It's the Scollays' idiot son!" I gasped.

I heard an exclamation both from Jean and the doctor.

"Son?" said Jean. "What! Did you think Jock was a Scollay?"

"He was sent up here about a couple of years ago to be looked after by these Scollays," explained the doctor. "We always supposed he was somebody's - ?" he glanced at Jean and hesitated - "er - somebody's son."

"Good Heavens!" I cried. "What a fool I've been!"

Swiftly I ran over in my mind my first night with the Scollay household. Had I ever been told Jock was a son? No, I had simply assumed it, and gone on that assumption without ever once thinking anything more about the matter. And so, with this impenetrable curtain between me and all possibility of guessing the truth I had gone on uselessly groping.

"Fool!"

A harsh voice startled me. It was Jock, gazing viciously up at me and talking guttural English now. His face was still framed in the circle of the torch, and as I looked at it now I realised that the truth had actually been written there all the time for a closely observing eye to read. This man's features differed vitally from the Scollays' and, especially, there was no cast in his eyes.

"Fool!" he snarled, "yes, you have been a damned fool, you Hobhouse! Ach, if I had known, you should have been a dead fool!"

"You mean if you hadn't been made a bit of a fool of too?" I suggested.

He was a brave man and a useful man to his country, but the German boastfulness would out.

"Ach, but I should have found you out soon! Me, you would have found out never!"

His eyes rolled round our party and I could see curiosity overcoming even his bragging.

"Who did tell you?" he demanded.

"If it is any satisfaction to you to know," replied Sir Francis, "your machinations were discovered and you were tracked down and caught by a girl." He turned to Jean and added, "An exceedingly clever, brave and patriotic girl."

I am sorry to say our prisoner still further smirched his record. What he said was fortunately in German and the words at the beginning of his sentence were not the kind that Jean would know. Before he had finished it my uncle had struck him with the butt end of the torch on the mouth.

"Hold your foul tongue!" he cried and then turned away and I could see a kind of shiver run over him.

"God forgive me!" he murmured. "I never struck a man when he was down before!" And then he recovered himself a little and added, "But is a German a human being?"

Meanwhile Jean was already bringing a bundle of rope from the corner under my cousin's direction, and in a few minutes his practised hands had knotted our prisoner up so securely that we were able to move aside from him and hold a hasty council of war.

"Now for the rest of the gang!" said my uncle. "Do you suppose they've heard us and bolted?"

"Do you mean the Scollays?" asked Jean. "Oh, I don't believe they knew!"

"My dear young lady, it's very painful for you to think your tenants are playing such games, but they simply must have known!"

"We can't afford to give them the benefit of the doubt," said Jack Whiteclett. "That's absolutely certain. I am afraid I must arrest them, Miss Rendall, and the sooner it's over the better."

"Jack!" commanded our uncle, "this is a matter I think I could handle rather better than a hot-headed young man." (Commander Whiteclett, it may be mentioned, was reputed in the Navy to have a remarkably cool head.) "Dr. Rendall, perhaps you will be good enough to keep watch over our prisoner for a few minutes while we are gone. Roger, give the doctor your pistol. If we hear you fire, doctor, we'll be out in a few seconds. Jack and Roger, come along with me."

Jack and I exchanged a look but said nothing. Our uncle still held the torch, and flashing it before him led the way out of the barn. We followed him, but my eyes I am afraid were over my shoulder. I saw Jean slip her own torch into the doctor's hand and then she ran after me.

"May I come too!" she whispered.

"Of course!" I said, "you're in command of the party - or ought to be!" and out we went together.

The farm yard made rough walking, and there seemed every excuse for my taking her arm and none for her objecting; nor did she.

"Who is this delightful, arbitrary old gentleman?" she asked in my ear. "You never introduced me!"

"Our uncle," I murmured back. "Jack and I both have expectations so we've got to give him his head!"

I must say Sir Francis stage-managed our entrance into the Scollays' house very effectively. As he quietly opened the door, he got us all close behind him, exactly like a band of robbers, so that we trod on one another's heels down a yard or two of narrow passage. The Scollays were all seated round the kitchen table when our uncle's figure suddenly towered out of the gloom, his pistol covering Peter senior's head, and his voice thundering:

"Hands up!"

At the first command they simply gasped.

"Hands up or I fire!" thundered Sir Francis again, and up went every pair of hands, and what is more they stayed up.

"Your confederate is captured and has confessed everything!" announced Sir Francis.

The family visibly trembled but looked more amazed than ever.

"This fellow they call - " My uncle looked over his shoulder and whispered, "What the devil was the fellow's name." And then in his stentorian voice again, "This fellow called Jock has confessed! So I know all about it. What have you got to say for yourselves?"

I saw their bewildered eyes wandering from one to the other of the family, and in a moment Mrs. Scollay asked in a quavering voice,

"What's come over Jock, do ye say, sir?"

"He has *confessed*!" repeated my uncle. "We know that he is a German spy!"

He glared at each astounded face in turn and then exclaimed over his shoulder,

"By Heaven, I actually don't believe they knew!"

J. Storer Clouston

"I think, sir, if you'll allow me," suggested my cousin, "I'd like to put a few questions."

"Well," growled our uncle, "fire away!"

We all trooped into the kitchen and the whole four of us cross-examined that family in turn, so that by the end of it we got a pretty good idea of how the land lay.

It seemed that two years before, the Scollays had been visited by a polite stranger apparently of the tourist species. This gentleman, after admiring the healthy yet retired situation of their residence, had suddenly been seized with an inspiration. The very place for an unfortunate young man of his acquaintance! he cried, and thereupon asked them if they could take charge of a blameless, helpless, harmless idiot. The stranger hinted that there were the best of reasons why the parents of this unfortunate wished him kept in the background. He had been boarded out previously, it appeared, but too near home, and now here was an ideal out-of-the-way spot for his retirement! The terms were so handsome that further enquiries on the Scollays' part seemed superfluous, and so in a week's time Jock had arrived.

His harmlessness had been absolutely guaranteed, provided always that no restraints were put upon him and that any little innocent fancy was indulged. Thus he wandered all over the island and at all hours, sometimes even wandering out at night when the foolish fancy took him, until this was accepted as the normal thing for harmless Jock. Another innocent whim he had of making a collection of rubbishy odds and ends and keeping them in a box in the barn. He had even repeated "Lock! Lock!" and stamped his harmless foot till they good-naturedly provided him with a lock and key for this treasure chest. And thus long before August, 1914, Jock was provided with a character that rendered his habits above suspicion, and a strong box which nobody would ever dream of examining.

Two or three times the same polite tourist paid a visit to the island to see how the poor demented young man was being looked after, and on these occasions he would take Jock out for quite a long walk, and afterwards assure the family that their guest's health was benefiting greatly. But this gentleman had not visited the island since the war, it seemed.

This was the Scollays' story and I think we all believed that in the main it was true. In fact, since then it has stood the test of all the evidence that could be got to check it. At the same time it seemed pretty clear that their greed had made them blinder than any one without a strong monetary interest could possibly have been. For fear of losing their little gold mine they had shut their eyes when people of average common sense would have opened them pretty wide. Our questions convicted them of this much, and at the end Whiteclett said emphatically that the two Peters must depart that night with him for further examination, if for nothing more.

"I'll leave you here with them, sir, for a moment, while I have a look at the other prisoner," he said quickly before our uncle could begin to issue the commands that we knew were coming, and with a sign to Jean and myself, hurried out.

We were at his heels and followed him to the barn.

There Jock was still lying bound with the doctor sitting over him.

"Has he said anything to you?" asked my cousin when he had called the doctor aside.

Dr. Rendall smiled under his grey moustache.

"He offered me £200 in gold to be paid on the nail if I would let him loose. We must have a dig for that money to-morrow, Whiteclett."

"Anything else?"

"Not a word after I had refused, and it's my belief you'll never get another word out of the man between now and his execution."

"He seems that sort," my cousin agreed. "And now, doctor, you and I will carry him into the house and keep Sir Francis company. The three of us will have an eye on all the prisoners then, till I can get some fellows up from the drifter to escort them. Do you mind going down to the boat, Roger, and sending up a party? You can find your way in the dark?"

"I'll make a shift to."

"Perhaps if Miss Rendall is going home she might put you on the right road," he suggested.

"Of course I will!" said Jean.

As I left him, Jack pressed my hand and whispered,

" Never say again I'm not tactful , Roger !

Congratulations, old chap, you've brought off a triple event if I'm not mistaken!"

"Triple?"

"That's one," he said pointing to our prisoner, "Uncle Francis is another, and I'll bet you sixpence I'm right about the third as soon as you shave that filthy beard. Get off with you now and don't keep a lady waiting!"

XVIII

THE FROSTY ROAD

Sometimes we walked and sometimes we trotted in step side by side, her arm through mine, where I had persuaded it to venture, and where it thrilled me by remaining. Personally I was not in the least anxious to bring our errand to an early end, but Jean was fired with zeal to astonish my relations by the speed with which we brought reinforcements, and so, trot and walk, we hurried down the frosted road through that black March night, talking, talking, almost every step of the way.

It was she who began as soon as we were clear of the farm.

"Are your uncle and Captain Whiteclett going back tonight?" she asked anxiously, and when I said I didn't know, she cried, "Well then I must come back and see them in case they go. There has been no time to explain and they must be told that it was simply my stupidity that prevented you from catching Jock sooner!"

"Your - what?" I exclaimed.

" Yes, I ought to have seen that you didn't know he

wasn't one of the family!" she insisted. "And that was one of the reasons why I went and interfered again when I'd vowed I wouldn't. I thought if you didn't suspect him, perhaps I was wrong, and if I had been, you'd never have trusted my 'guesses' again; so I wanted to get some proof to show you. But all the credit is really yours."

Our debate on this point was too one-sided to be worth recording. And yet though my arguments were irresistible, she would persist - and persists to this day - that somehow or other I unmasked Jock the spy.

"Well, let's leave it at that," I said at last. "Disguised as Miss Rendall, alone I did it! And now tell me what made you suspect the man?"

"It was only when you told me about meeting him by the cliffs on the day of the murder that I suddenly thought of Bolton's discovery and then I saw that he must have meant Jock. At least I guessed, but I knew it would seem the wildest idea until there was a little more proof, and so I determined to make a few enquiries and then tell you at once if there seemed to be anything in my idea. So next morning I went to the Scollays and paid them a friendly visit and began talking about Jock and his habits and movements, and I found he had disappeared for a good part of that day when Bolton was murdered. I also found he was often out at nights, and that he kept that locked box in the barn."

"So you felt sure?"

"I would have if you hadn't made me rather less confident about my guesses. Still, I'd have told you next morning, only when you showed me that pocket-book you seemed so positive that you quite shook me. And then I determined to go myself and break into the box and see if I could find some proof."

"That's the one thing I can't quite forgive you for; running all that risk by yourself!"

"But that was just the point! I had somehow got it into my head that since I had found you out, perhaps he had too, and I remembered what happened to Bolton, and I couldn't let you run the risk when it was quite safe for me!"

"Quite safe!" I exclaimed. "Quite safe if he had caught you opening his box?"

"Oh, one has to run a *little* risk," she admitted. "But I knew unless he actually caught me he would never suspect me."

"Well," I said, "every one has his own idea of what's a soft job. But you did think it worth wiring for my cousin?"

"Believe me," she said earnestly, "I only really decided to do that after you had gone back and I couldn't consult you! I did *think* of it while you were with me, but you were so positive that there was no need for wiring that I thought you might absolutely refuse to let me in any case - "

"And so you decided to decide after I had gone? I see! Well, all I can say is I have been very judiciously handled."

"You are frightfully good-natured!" she declared, apparently in all sincerity.

I had given up debating my virtues by this time.

"It's this sea air," I said modestly, and enjoyed the delicious sensation of trying to see her smile in the dark, and imagining how sweet she would look if it were lighter.

Going over each incident together as we hurried down the island that night, I was glad to find, however, one part of my conduct which events had thoroughly justified. If on that first night I had not instantly assumed the role of a fellow Hun, I assuredly should not have been walking with Jean Rendall now. Undoubtedly I had kept my enemy thinking up till that unfortunate Sunday afternoon when I had made my fatal blunder of trying to enlist the gabbling Jock as an ally, or I should have been dead long before then.

"You guessed right," I said. "That was when I gave myself away - only it was not to any one behind a wall! And do you know I believe the fellow actually tried me with the proper answer for the sheep riddle, only I could make nothing out of it. Was I an idiot, or would any one have done the same?"

"Any one!" she said with conviction. "And don't you think I was right now about the reason why he stopped firing next day?"

"I begin to think you were. He was cunning enough to see that it wasn't worth while running any risks, when he could probably get a sitting shot next time. And he would have got me if you hadn't arrested me. Heavens!

To think of that man single-handed defying the British Navy and the British Police and actually making it impossible for any pursuer he considered dangerous to remain alive in this island! Bolton went, poor chap, and I would have gone but for you."

Perhaps I pressed her arm a little. Anyhow, she answered nothing for a moment, and then in a low voice said,

"Poor Bolton! Oh, you've no idea how frightened I got that morning when I heard the news!"

I knew it was not for herself she was frightened, and my heart beat quicker.

"I wonder how it happened," she went on. "I've often wondered since!"

"If I may venture to guess too," I said, "I should say that Bolton was undoubtedly on the right track. He had found that Jock was not one of the family and had got suspicious of his movements, but one may safely take it Jock was watching him like a cat watching a mouse - very likely he managed to overhear Bolton making enquiries, and he deliberately laid a scent for him that took him to the cliffs."

"That sounds very likely," said she. "And then he took Bolton's pocket book and made those entries."

"That pocket book is rather a sore subject!" I said.

I heard a little gurgle of laughter, but then she did not know how sore the subject was. My scene with the unfortunate doctor was hardly my happiest recollection of Ransay.

And so we went on trotting and walking and talking, and all the time I was realising more and more vividly that if this could only be made the first of ten thousand evenings with her, I should be the luckiest man in the world. Also I was realising that for some reason she seemed to think I had done something rather heroic in returning to the place where I had nearly been scythed and shot, and tackling the unknown enemy single-handed; especially after she happened to discover I had been wounded. It made me feel - well, a little abashed and dreadfully afraid of being found out when she knew me better, but extraordinarily happy for the moment.

But for one sobering fact I should have told her everything I felt and hoped before that walk was over. The beard of Thomas Sylvester Hobhouse still wagged between us. Till I had got rid of that black hirsute horror I was not going to risk my chances of happiness. It was pitch dark, I admit, but then in certain delicate situations, well, if I were a girl I should strongly object, especially if I knew it were dyed and didn't know if the dye would run.

And so we sent up the reinforcements, and then I saw her home, and hurried back myself with a dancing heart to meet the others.

J. Storer Clouston

XIX

OUR MORNING CALL

John Whiteclett and the three prisoners went aboard at once, but the doctor and I easily persuaded my uncle to spend the night with us. He was very stiff, poor old boy, after his exertions, and went early to bed, but I had a busy night of it. With the aid of the doctor's razors and the doctor's medical skill I finally got rid of the beard and the dye about 2 a.m. and went to sleep a clean-shaved blonde once more.

During breakfast next morning, I noticed more than once my uncle's eyes fixed on me in a very significant way, and Dr. Rendall seemed to notice it too, for when breakfast was over he tactfully left us to ourselves.

"H'm, you have lost no time in making yourself look like a Christian again, I notice," my uncle began.

"I lost no time in beginning, sir, but I assure you it was a devilish stiff conversion."

"And what was your hurry, Roger?"

"Anxiety to do you credit, Uncle Francis."

" You are becoming a dutiful nephew damned

suddenly," observed Sir Francis.

"It has come on during this lonely life," I explained.

"In that case what shall we do with ourselves this morning? Revisit the scene of last night's affair, eh?"

"I thought a walk in the other direction might give you a better idea of this interesting island," I suggested.

"Is there anything to see in the other direction?" he enquired, still with the same gravity, but with an eye that inadvertently twinkled every now and then.

"I thought of presenting you to the proprietor of the island, sir."

My uncle looked at me fixedly for a moment and then abruptly enquired:

"Do you mean to marry her, Roger?"

"That's entirely for her to say, Uncle Francis."

"Well, you'll be deuced lucky if she says 'yes'! By the way, what are you going to marry on?"

This was a somewhat delicate question but I thought it best to be candid.

"The advertised reward," I replied.

"For what, may I ask?"

"For catching the spy."

"Oh, *you* claim that!"

"No, she does."

My uncle smiled beneficently.

"That's all right, old fellow," said he, "and I'll intimate as much to her father. Come on! Now you've shaved, what are you waiting for?"

"Your blessing, sir; but I'm ready now."

The very weather was encouraging, for the wind had fallen considerably, and it was just cold enough to make us step out over the frozen road in bursting spirits. My uncle literally whistled several times, and once he remarked *à propos* of nothing:

"I've always admired that type myself!"

On what decent pretext I managed to get Jean out of the library within two minutes of her entrance with her father, or whether it actually was decent, my memory is a blank. I knew she loved me because she came out with me so quickly, and she knew my heart because I asked her to. And as we both had really known the night before, there scarcely needed a question to be asked and answered. And that is the end of Jean's and my part in the story.

* * * * *

As for that brave, brutal and extraordinary man who had masqueraded as an imbecile for two whole years to serve the ambitions of his country, playing the part of a kind of isolated living base for the German Navy, as a spy, as a destroyer, and as a murderer, I have never learned his name or his past history to this day. After his first outburst of blasphemy, I believe he kept doggedly silent up to his speedy end. He lived and died like a savage, cunning, carnivorous beast; or, in other words, like his masters who employed him.